Tua was trying to imagine it smaller, as if a smaller elephant would be easier to hide than a larger one. But whenever she managed to squeeze it in a box smaller than itself (in her mind, that is), the elephant flapped its ears (knocking the lid off of that imaginary box) and out came its trunk.

Tua wanted to say, "Could you please put that thing away, *chang*?" but she was afraid it might sound impolite. Besides, where does an elephant put its trunk when it isn't using it? It doesn't have a pocket or a purse to put it in. And you might well ask, when does an elephant *not* use its trunk? An elephant's trunk is always doing something.

The very next thought that stumbled into Tua's mind was: What am I going to tell my mother?

She imagined herself saying, "Mama, guess what I found?"

That might work with a kitten or a puppy, but it wasn't going to work with an elephant. And how would she get it up the apartment stairs? Where would it sleep? What does an elephant eat?

Taking the elephant home was definitely out of the question.

Tua
and the
Elephant

By R. P. HARRIS
Illustrated by TAEEUN YOO

chronicle books · san francisco

For Mishy—R. P. H.

First paperback edition published in 2013 by Chronicle Books LLC.
Originally published in hardcover in 2012 by Chronicle Books LLC.

ISBN 978-1-4521-2703-3

The Library of Congress has cataloged the original edition as follows:

Harris, R. P. (Randal Perry)
  Tua and the elephant / by Randal Harris ; illustrated by Taeeun Yoo.
    p. cm.
  ISBN 978-0-8118-7781-7 (alk. paper)
 1. Asiatic elephant—Juvenile fiction. 2. Animal rescue—Juvenile fiction. 3. Animal
welfare—Juvenile fiction. 4. Animal sanctuaries—Juvenile fiction. 5. Chiang Mai (Thailand)—Juvenile fiction. [1. Asiatic elephant—Fiction. 2. Elephants—Fiction. 3. Animal
rescue—Fiction. 4. Animals—Treatment—Fiction. 5. Animal sanctuaries—Fiction. 6.
Chiang Mai (Thailand)—Fiction. 7. Thailand—Fiction.] I. Yoo, Taeeun, ill. II. Title.
PZ7.H24349Tu 2012
813.6——dc23

2011030675

Manufactured in China.

MIX
Paper from
responsible sources
FSC
www.fsc.org   FSC™ C101537

Book design by ELOISE LEIGH.
Cover illustration by TAEEUN YOO.
Typeset in Dederon Serif.
The illustrations in this book were rendered in charcoal, linoleum block print, and
Photoshop.

10 9 8 7 6 5 4 3 2

Chronicle Books LLC
680 Second Street, San Francisco, California 94107

Chronicle Books—we see things differently. Become part of our community at
www.chroniclekids.com.

Prologue

When Tua was born, a nurse in the delivery room exclaimed, "Look at the little peanut!" *Tua*, in Thai, means peanut. And Tua, having arrived prematurely, was quite small. At that exact moment, she let out such a scream for attention that all of the doctors and nurses in the delivery room exhaled sighs of relief. It was clear that this baby, small though she was, was a survivor. She had just ordered them to get on with the job of making her comfortable, and that is exactly what they did. Soon everyone in the maternity ward was calling the little baby in the incubator Tua.

And that is how she got her name.

CHAPTER ONE

In the Night Market

Tua and her mother lived in Chiang Mai, Thailand, on a quiet lane near one of the city's most popular night markets.

"Tua, darling, where are you? I need your help. My shoes have run off, and I'm late for work."

Tua leapt up from her desk and ran to fetch her mother's shoes from outside the front door.

"Wherever did you find them? I looked everywhere."

"They were on the porch," Tua said.

"Were they running away or sneaking back home?"

"They were where you left them when you came home from work," she reminded her mother. "Like you always do."

Suay Nam hugged and kissed her daughter, then slipped on her shoes. "What *would* I do without you? Oh, I'm late! What time is it? I gotta go. I love you the most!"

"I love you the most," Tua called down the stairs.

"If you need anything, go to Auntie Orchid's. And don't stay out too late at the night market. Have you got the number of the restaurant?"

"I've got it," Tua said.

As soon as her mother was out of sight, Tua put away her homework and dashed into the street as if late for an appointment of her own.

"*Sawatdee kha*, Uncle," Tua said to Somchai, the roti pancake vendor.

"Who speaks?" Somchai called over his cart.

"It's me, Tua," Tua said, stretching to the tips of her toes and waving her hand in the air.

"Of course it is, who else could it be?" Somchai replied, handing Tua a banana roti with chocolate sauce and condensed milk.

"*Khawp khun kha.*" Tua politely thanked him.

"How's your mother?"

"She's working at the restaurant tonight," Tua said, and took a greedy bite of the banana roti.

"Always working. Every day and every night." Somchai stretched his neck like a tortoise and sighed. "Some of us were only born to work."

"I'm going to the night market," Tua said.

"Don't let me keep you from your appointed rounds, then. Better play while you may."

"*Kha.*" Tua waved good-bye and zigzagged through the clogged traffic to the other side of the street.

"Hey, Tua, what's your big hurry?" Uncle Khun the *tuk-tuk* driver called out as she skipped onto the curb. He was collapsed in the back of his three-wheeled taxi, with one bare leg dangling over the side like a python.

"I'm going to the night market," Tua pouted. But recalling her mother's warning, "Girls who pout bite their cheeks," she immediately unpuckered her face.

"Get in," Khun winked. "I'll give you a good price."

"No thank you," she said. "I'm almost there."

Khun threw back his head to laugh, thought better of it, pulled a newspaper over his face, and fell asleep to a lullaby of honking horns, screeching tires, and the occasional collision.

The alley Tua ducked down, *soi* 5, led her to the middle of the night market. She stopped at the end with hands on hips, surveying her domain as if waiting for a cue to enter the stage.

Strings of bare lightbulbs crisscrossed overhead, igniting the street in a blaze. Vendors' carts crowded both sides of the street, hawking their wares to the people strolling down the middle.

Curries with rice and curries with noodles; *pad Thai* and *pad Thai* omelets; rotis with chocolate sauce and condensed milk; sticky rice and mango; green papaya salad with shredded carrots, tomatoes, green onions, and peanuts. Taro, tamarind, durian, and coconut ice cream, and crispy banana fritters. Sliced watermelon, pineapple, papaya, and mango nestled on beds of crushed ice. Coconut oil sizzled in woks, grills smoked, and blenders whirred.

A traditional band made up of a coconut-shell fiddle, bamboo flute, skin drum, chimes, gongs, and a wooden xylophone competed with a boy dancing to pop music on a screeching boom box. A girl in a school uniform scratched out a tune on a battered violin.

"*Sawatdee khrap*, Tua," said a bare-chested boy as he hung a string of jasmine flowers around her neck. White jasmine necklaces climbed up the length of his arm.

"*Khawp khun kha*, Ananda," she thanked him, lifting the string of flowers to her nose and inhaling the sugary-sweet scent.

Lam, Ananda's sister, tugged at Tua's elbow. Tua lifted the girl in her arms and rubbed noses with her.

Tua nodded at the dozens of jasmine necklaces around her neck. "You smell good enough to eat. Are you going to sell all of those tonight?"

Lam shook her head no, then nodded yes.

"Come, Lam," Ananda said. He reached for his sister, sat her down, and took her by the hand. "See you later, Tua!"

"*Kha*." Tua waved good-bye and stepped into the strolling current.

Halfway through the market, Tua stopped to watch a man carve a bar of soap into the shape of an elephant when she heard a voice call out behind her.

"Does the little peanut want a foot massage?"

Tua spun around and searched the rows of people on mats having their muscles and limbs pummeled and pulled until she spotted Auntie Duan, the blind masseuse.

"*Sawatdee kha*, Auntie. How did you know it was me?"

"By the sound of your footsteps."

"But it's too noisy to hear my footsteps," Tua argued.

"Then I must have smelled you," Duan shrugged.

Tua still wasn't convinced. "What do I smell like?"

"Night jasmine and chocolate sauce," guessed Auntie Duan.

Tua opened her mouth but was too flabbergasted to speak.

"Tua, don't just stand there with your mouth hanging open like a carp," hollered Auntie Nam, the curry noodle vendor. "Run over to Uncle Sip's and fetch me some bean sprouts. And don't let the old bandit cheat you," she warned, flipping a ten-*baht* coin into Tua's hands.

"*Kha*," Tua said, after closing her mouth and inspecting the coin. Then she leapt into the market like a cat, weaving her way through and around the legs of the shoppers until she came to a stop in front of Uncle Sip's vegetable stand.

"*Sawatdee kha*, Uncle."

"What's that?" he barked, still angry with the chef who had offered such a ridiculously low price for his cabbages. Some people didn't seem to know that life is a wheel, and that every living thing is only a spoke in the wheel of life.

"Life is a wheel, Tua," Uncle Sip declared suddenly, as if the idea had just occurred to him.

"And we are only spokes in the wheel of life, Uncle."

This response brought Sip out of his reverie. He looked down at Tua and grinned like a gecko.

"You are so smart, Tua. Who taught you that?"

"You did, Uncle."

"No wonder you're so smart, then. Did you finish your homework?"

"*Kha*," Tua said, crossing her fingers behind her back. "All finished."

"Good. That's good, because you'll never get ahead in this world on night market philosophy alone. You need an education. Let's test your math and haggling skills. Pretend you're here to do some shopping."

"But I *am* here to do some shopping. I need bean sprouts for Auntie Nam."

"Pretend you've come on an errand to buy bean sprouts for Auntie Nam," Sip suggested, as if this, too, was an original idea.

"Ten *baht* a pound," he announced.

Tua handed him the ten-*baht* coin.

"You're supposed to haggle," he whispered.

"May I have some change, please?"

Uncle Sip handed Tua a bag of bean sprouts and a five-*baht* coin.

"Good. Very good indeed," he said. "Well-mannered and forthright. Manners are harder to teach than business skills. We'll work on the haggling tomorrow."

"*Kha*, Uncle," Tua said, and shot off back to Auntie Nam.

Auntie Nam plucked the bag of bean sprouts out of Tua's hands and replaced it with a bowl of curry noodles.

"Yum, Auntie!" Tua said. "I love *khao soi*."

Auntie Nam held out the flat of her hand while Tua, balancing the hot bowl in one tiny palm like a juggler, dropped the five-*baht* coin into it. Auntie Nam squeezed her eyes into slits and stared down at the coin with suspicion, sniffed approval at last, pocketed it, and brushed her hand affectionately across Tua's cheek.

"Good girl," she said. "Now eat."

"*Kha*, Auntie," Tua said, and sat down on a little plastic stool that seemed custom-made for a girl her size.

"*Aroy mak mak*," she said, expressing her pleasure to the bowl of *khao soi* in her lap. The aroma rose up from it in a spicy cloud that encircled her head and poured into her nostrils, filling her with a warm and comforting glow.

She might have remained in that trance had Auntie Nam not dropped a handful of crispy fried noodles into Tua's bowl and squeezed half a lime over the top of them. The gesture broke the spell Tua was in, and she lifted the bowl to her lips with both hands and drank the rich, thick curry sauce. "It's so delicious!" she repeated, this time to Auntie Nam instead of the bowl.

Auntie Nam bowed a *wai* with her palms pressed together, thanking Tua for the compliment.

After washing her bowl and spoon, and all of the other bowls and spoons that needed washing, Tua bid good luck to Auntie Nam and continued on her rounds. She stopped for a gossip and a giggle with her school chum Kip, who, with her mother, Na, sold hand-painted paper umbrellas, silks, sarongs, and Thai fisherman pants. When Na called Kip back to work, Tua began following a scruffy brown dog with a muzzle over his snout.

"Why are you wearing that muzzle?" she asked the brown dog.

The brown dog led Tua to a quiet corner of the market. Then he settled down on his haunches beside a large, teetering pile of boxes and crates, and tugged at the muzzle with his front paws.

"Would you like me to help you take that off?" she asked him.

The brown dog lifted his ears, tilted his head in an attitude of welcome surprise as if to say, "What an especially good idea," and attempted as best he could to affect a grin behind the muzzle.

"First you must tell me why you're wearing it," Tua said.

But before he could speak, if speech is possible for a brown dog with a muzzle on his snout, a slim gray cat dropped from the sky (or perhaps from the wall separating the market from the street) and onto the boxes and crates. The cat glared down at the brown dog, then snarled and hissed—rather rudely, Tua thought. The dog must have thought it rude as well, for he leapt up from his crouch, sending the boxes, crates, and the gray cat scattering.

That was as good an answer to the question of why he was wearing a muzzle as Tua could have gotten from the brown dog himself, muzzle or no muzzle. It was a mystery unlocked.

But now, there in the wall, a new mystery presented itself. Behind where the boxes and crates had been stacked higher than a brown dog can jump—and gaping like old Grandma Orn's toothless mouth—there, looking just big enough for Tua to squeeze through . . . was a hole.

If walls could talk, this one would have invited Tua to step through the hole to the other side.

CHAPTER TWO

The Other Side of the Wall

Tua put her foot through the hole as if testing her weight on the outer limb of a tree.

"I'll just have a look," she said.

Then, with a backward glance, she squeezed the rest of herself through. Straightening up to her full height on the other side, she cast her eyes about the busy street.

The buildings were taller and grander (some of them even had names), and they seemed to lean over the sidewalk as if inspecting the traffic, human and motorized, before selecting who or what they would direct inside them. They often chose badly, or so it seemed to Tua, for they spit out as many through one door as they admitted through another.

"Perhaps they can't make up their minds," Tua supposed. "There are just too many people and cars and motorbikes to choose from."

And it was while she was musing on the flighty nature of large buildings that she found herself caught up in a current of pedestrian traffic. Tua didn't attempt to struggle out of this current any more than a leaf caught in a flooding gutter would have done, but allowed it to take her where it would.

Before long she found herself in a crowd of unfamiliar people, all of whom were much taller than she—so tall, as it happened, that they blocked from view the landmarks she used to navigate the city by. When this human current stopped at last, she tugged on the nearest sleeve to beg assistance.

"*Kho thot kha*," Tua said, begging the woman's pardon.

But the face that looked down from the sleeve she was tugging was not a Thai face. It was a *farang* face.

A *farang* is a creature from a foreign land. It can be from France, or Germany, or Ireland, or

England, or Sweden, or Fiji, or Italy, or Australia, or New Zealand, or Uruguay, or even the United States of America. Tua had seen many *farangs* before, but she'd never actually met one. *Farangs*, unless they are unusually clever, don't speak Thai. The *farang* whose sleeve Tua had been tugging was unusual in appearance only.

"Oh, hullo, honey," the big-nosed *farang* said, lifting her bug-eyed sunglasses and leaning over Tua.

Tua leaned back on her heels. "*Sawatdee kha*," she replied.

"I'm afraid I don't have any small change for you, darling," she said, and patted Tua on the top of the head.

Tua bunched her fists and twisted her mouth into a frown. It is taboo and impolite to touch a Thai on the top of the head. The top of the head is the highest part of the body, spiritually as well as physically.

"Frowns pinch the heart," she remembered her mother saying, and immediately unwrinkled her face.

"Oh, all right, dearie," the *farang* said impatiently as she gave Tua a twenty-*baht* note and dismissed her with a fluttering hand.

Tua recalled what Uncle Sip had so often said about *farangs*: that they were under the misapprehension that they were the wheel of life itself rather than spokes like everyone—and everything—else. "*Farangs* are as noisy as frogs in a pond," he was fond of saying. "And puffed up to twice their normal size."

A twenty-*baht* note is nothing to scoff at. It would buy four pounds of bean sprouts for one with bargaining skills. But Tua had no use for it. She no more needed money than a chicken needs teeth. Sometimes possessing nothing is like having everything.

That was why she began to cast her eyes about for someone to share this small fortune with. But she was still imprisoned in a forest of legs and hips and stomachs.

Suddenly, like a train leaving a station, this mass of body parts lurched forward on the signal of the changing light, and carried its prisoner, Tua, with it.

Escape through the scissoring legs was impossible, and weaving around them only produced more legs, hips, buttocks, and stomachs. This mass of legs would stop from time to time, collapse into itself, pull apart again, and continue on its many-legged way, like a giant caterpillar.

"*Kho thot kha*," excuse me, Tua said as she tugged the back pocket in front of her. "You're crushing me."

"Thief!" the pocket cried out in alarm. "Pick-pocket!"

Those four syllables had the power of an incantation, for no sooner had they been spoken than the legs and their attachments scurried away in all directions like ants fleeing a monsoon.

Tua found herself standing alone in an open square beside a fountain. This was not a fountain

Tua had ever seen before. She turned in a slow circle, scanning the skyline in search of a familiar landmark. And just as she was about to swallow the lump in her throat, she swung her head back to the gray blur that her eyes had bumped over: something vaguely, fuzzily familiar.

CHAPTER THREE

Tua Encounters an Elephant

"It's an elephant!" Tua cried out, and rudely pointed her finger.

The moment she saw the elephant swing its trunk and flap its ears, her fears and doubts evaporated.

All Thais love the elephant, from the beloved king in his palace to the monk in his temple; from the baby in the crib to the granny in the hammock; from the *tuk-tuk* driver to the roti vendor; from the city dweller to the rice farmer. And Tua, being Thai from her toenails to the part in her shiny black hair, was no exception. Tua loved elephants.

Of course, Tua had seen elephants before. Elephants make an appearance in Chiang Mai from time to time to entertain the tourists or participate in some ceremony or another. But there was something about this elephant that was different.

For a start, it was young like Tua—but it was still plenty big, even so. Some elephants are so big that one is reluctant to approach them. They are bigger than cars, bigger than trucks, bigger than buses—at least the wild ones are, or so Tua had been led to believe. (Whoever had led Tua to believe this, she could not remember; so it is probably safe to say that she led herself to believe that wild elephants were bigger than buses.)

But Tua was not the least bit afraid of this elephant. The first thought that entered her mind was: I must go and introduce myself. She had an overwhelming desire to tell it all about herself, certain that it would be just as delighted to meet her.

What stopped her were the two mahouts.

A master mahout becomes one with his elephant. He is brother and sister, mother and father, and son and daughter to his elephant. He lives, eats, and sleeps with his elephant. He feeds it from his table, and bathes with it in the river. The mahout becomes an elephant, and the elephant becomes a mahout. The two are inseparable.

But just as there are all kinds of elephants, so, too, there are all kinds of mahouts. And these two mahouts were as scruffy as sewer rats, beady eyed and sharp of tooth. Whiskers grew in sparse patches on their cheeks and chins like mildew. They were both shifty, but one was long and lean, and the other was squat and pudgy.

There was something about the way the elephant turned its head from side to side and eyeballed the two mahouts that gave Tua pause. And when it caught her gaze, she very nearly tumbled over backward. It was as if it were speaking to her with its eye.

She sat down on the steps of the fountain to give this situation a bit more study and thought.

The short mahout was holding out plastic bags of sliced pineapple and watermelon to some *farangs* who, in turn, gave the fruit to the elephant. Nothing alarming about that, Tua thought. The *farangs* gave their money to the elephant, the elephant gave the money to the tall mahout, the short mahout gave the fruit to the *farangs*, and the *farangs* gave the fruit to the elephant. It is how the market economy works. But she recalled how Uncle Sip had told her that free trade was freer for some than it was for others, so Tua watched this business transaction more closely. And that was a good thing, too, for the elephant then did something extraordinary— even for an elephant.

After accepting a fifty-*baht* note from a *farang*, taking it with its trunk as easily as someone with an opposable thumb and four fingers, the elephant stretched as far as it could reach and dropped the note in the lap of a woman who, motioning with hand to mouth in a pantomime of hunger, sat begging on the street with her baby.

Both mahouts bristled like cats.

"Oh, thank you, *chang*, thank you." The woman bowed her head to the pavement.

The *farangs* grinned nervously, clutched their bags, and reared back on their heels.

"Oh my," said the short one.

"My goodness," said the tall one.

"How sad," said the one in between.

The mahouts snorted and snickered, as if to reassure the *farangs* that it was all part of the show.

"Did you see that, Nak?" said the short one. "The elephant gave our money away."

Nak, the tall one, glared at the poor woman, and then smiled at the *farangs*. "Don't give them any more fruit, Nang. We're closed for business."

After the *farangs* had gone, the two mahouts scolded the elephant and tugged its ears. Then they went over to the woman and, when they thought no one was looking, snatched all of the notes and coins in her lap.

"Have pity," she pleaded, shielding her baby. "Have mercy."

Deaf to her cries, the mahouts walked away with her money, wrapped a heavy chain around the elephant's neck, and attempted to lead it off. But the elephant refused to budge. Instead, it turned toward Tua and once again held her gaze.

"Did you see that?" it seemed to say.

It wasn't until Tua nodded her head and mouthed the words, "Yes, *chang*, I saw," that the elephant allowed itself to be taken away.

Tua hopped off the top step of the fountain like a cricket; ran over to the poor woman and handed her the twenty-*baht* note the *farang* had given her; bowed respectfully, palms together in a *wai*; and scampered after the elephant.

CHAPTER FOUR

The Elephant Beckons

Tua's eyes fixed on the elephant: its swaying rump and its swishing tail. The tail seemed to beckon like a wave—like a curling finger. From time to time the elephant looked around its shoulder to see if she was still following. As the streets became alleys, and the alleys became paths, it grew darker and darker. Still Tua followed the switching tail.

"Come," the tail beckoned. "It's only a little farther."

"Forward, brute!" Nak barked, as he struck the elephant's hind leg with a bamboo stick. "Give my money away, will you? We'll see about that. No money; no dinner." And he struck the elephant again.

"I'm hungry," said Nang. "What's for dinner?"

"You're drinking it," answered Nak, and he passed a bottle behind the elephant's rump.

Nang drained the contents and tossed the bottle back over his shoulder. It exploded with a crash near Tua's feet.

"What was that?" Nak spun around, squinted his eyes, and cocked his ears.

"Just the bottle," Nang shrugged. "It was empty."

"Not that, you buckethead. Back there." He pointed to the banana tree that Tua had ducked behind.

"I don't see anything."

As Nang peered into the darkness, the elephant lurched forward and jerked him by the chain.

"Whoa, there, you." He stumbled backward. "Where do you think you're going?" He struck the elephant another blow and followed after.

The elephant seemed to take no notice of these beatings. Its only concern was whether Tua was still following.

They came at last to a beach beside the River Ping, where the mahouts had made their camp. Nak attached the end of the chain to a stake in the ground while Nang built a fire. As the fire burst into flames on the shore, its reflection did the same on the river. Tua threw herself behind a log to hide from the sudden blaze of light. Trapped until the flames died down and the mahouts retired to their tent, Tua curled up behind the log, closed her eyes, and promptly fell asleep.

A chill woke Tua as if a cold, wet hand had reached out and shaken her awake. How long had she been asleep?

She slowly raised her head and peeked over the top of the log. The fire had burned down to glowing embers and the mahouts were nowhere to be seen. The elephant stood at the end of its chain, with its shackled foot extended in the air behind it, as if it were trying to pull the stake out of the ground.

"Hello, *chang*," Tua whispered. She was about to ask if she could help, when she read the words in its eyes: "There you are! What have you been doing?"

"*Kho thot kha.* I'm sorry, *chang*," she whispered. "I'm coming."

Tua rose up, crept over to the tent, peeled back the flaps, and looked inside.

Both mahouts were fast asleep and snoring beside two empty bottles. A large pile of dung sat on the ground outside the tent flaps, like a trap. Tua looked back over her shoulder at the elephant.

"Don't look at me," the elephant's eyes seemed to say to her. "Now get this chain off my foot so we can get out of here."

"*Kha, chang*," she whispered. "Don't worry. I'm coming."

And that is how Tua found herself on the streets of Chiang Mai in the company of a fugitive elephant.

CHAPTER FIVE

Sizing Up the Elephant

Where does one take an elephant—a fugitive elephant, at that—in the city of Chiang Mai? How does one hide an elephant? Elephants don't fit into closets, boxes, or drawers. One can't simply toss a blanket over an elephant and call it a job well done. Someone is bound to notice. Elephants, for better or for worse, draw attention to themselves.

After they had crept far enough away from the camp for Tua to feel safe enough to catch her breath and collect her thoughts, she looked the elephant over as if trying to gauge its true shape, weight, and height. She was trying to imagine it smaller, as if a smaller elephant would be easier to hide than a larger one. But whenever she managed to squeeze it in a box smaller than itself (in her mind, that is), the elephant flapped its ears (knocking the lid off of that imaginary box) and out came its trunk.

Tua wanted to say, "Could you please put that thing away, *chang*?" but she was afraid it might sound impolite. Besides, where does an elephant put its trunk when it isn't using it? It doesn't have a pocket or a purse to put it in. And you might well ask, when does an elephant *not* use its trunk? An elephant's trunk is never completely at rest. It reaches with it, like an arm. It grasps with it, like a hand. It breathes and smells with it, like a nose. An elephant's trunk is always doing something.

The very next thought that stumbled into Tua's mind was: What am I going to tell my mother?

She imagined herself saying, "Mama, guess what I found?"

That might work with a kitten or a puppy, but it wasn't going to work with an elephant. And how would she get it up the apartment stairs? Where would it sleep? What does an elephant eat?

Taking the elephant home was definitely out of the question.

"I know!" Tua gasped. "I'll take you to my Auntie Orchid. She'll know what to do, she's an actress. Plus she's got a yard and a garden," she added as an afterthought, trying to assure the elephant that she had its best interests at heart. And also that she was of sound mind and judgment, a girl with big ideas.

The elephant gripped Tua's shoulder with its trunk and, turning her away from the river, gave her a gentle nudge as if to say: "That's nice. Now let's get a move on, shall we?"

"Okay, *chang*, I'm ready," Tua called back over her shoulder.

CHAPTER SIX

Meeting Auntie Orchid

After following the River Ping in the dark, Tua found her bearings and led the elephant down back alleys and unlit streets until she came to *soi* four, where her auntie lived.

"Wait here, *chang*," Tua said.

She stepped out of the shadows and knocked gently on the back door, imagining what she was going to say to her auntie. But before she had time to rehearse a speech, the door flew open and Auntie Orchid was standing in its place, wearing a red silk robe and green cold cream all over her face.

"Tu-*ah*!" she sang out, as if calling her in for supper. "What *are* you doing here?" she asked

suddenly, as if she couldn't remember inviting her over. "It's late," she declared. But that made it sound like she had invited her over and Tua was late in arriving. "Well, it's not that late, I suppose," she decided. "Come in, if you're coming."

"*Kha*, Auntie." Tua bowed a *wai*, glanced over her shoulder, and stepped into the house.

"Was I expecting you?" Auntie Orchid asked as she closed the door behind Tua, thinking it best for both parties if she got this matter sorted once and for all.

"I have an elephant," Tua said, ignoring the question. Then she began to relate the story of how she had rescued an elephant from a pair of rogues who were mistreating it, how they had stolen money from a poor woman and her baby, and what else was she to do?

"That's nice, darling," Auntie Orchid yawned. "Every girl should have a 'special friend.'" The yawn reminded Orchid that it was quite late after all.

"*Kha*, Auntie. Can I show it to you?"

"I don't know. *Can* you?"

"I mean, may I show it to you?"

"Yes, you may," said Auntie Orchid, "if you must."

Tua opened the door and gestured with her head for her auntie to look outside. The elephant had moved out of the shadows and was standing on the porch, its trunk curled in front of its face as if it were about to knock on the door.

"See?" Tua turned back to her auntie.

Auntie Orchid clasped her hands to the sides of her head and flung open her mouth as if to scream . . . but she didn't. She stretched out her leg and gently closed the door with her foot instead.

"Tua, darling," she calmly asked, "would you please tell me *why* . . . there is an *elephant* standing on MY . . . back . . . porch?"

"I told you already, Auntie. There were two bad men being mean to the elephant and it asked me to help so I followed it to the river and—"

"All right, all right, I remember now. Slow down. Take a deep breath." Auntie Orchid inhaled deeply, following her own advice. "First of all," she continued, "that elephant is not an it; she's a she."

"It is? How do you know?"

Tua hadn't considered the possibility that the elephant was a she. It was an elephant. But now it was a she—like she was. Tua wanted to open the door and look at it—look at her—again.

"I know because I am a country girl. That is, I *was* a country girl. Of course now I'm Lady Orchid, 'The Lotus of the North.' And 'Chiang Mai's First Lady of Sooong' (she trilled musically), 'Comedy' (she grinned toothily), 'and Tragedy'" (she frowned forlornly). At the conclusion of this performance, she took an extravagant bow.

"I grew up in the country, and I know elephants." With that, she flung open the back door and leaned out to look the elephant in the eyes.

"Look at that face! Isn't she lovely?" Auntie Orchid batted her eyelashes at the elephant, perhaps a little enviously (for elephants have very long and beautiful eyelashes). Then she turned to

Tua and added: "But that doesn't mean she can come in the house."

"No, of course not, Auntie." Tua shook her head. "Where should we put her, then?"

Auntie Orchid imagined trying to explain to her neighbors why there was an elephant in her backyard.

"Alright," she sighed, "but not in the bedroom. And we had better put down some newspaper," she added with a shudder.

"Come in, *chang*," Tua said. She was already thinking that she needed to give the elephant a name.

CHAPTER SEVEN

An Elephant by Any Other Name

An elephant on the porch is not the same thing as an elephant in the kitchen. Elephants seem to grow larger indoors, somehow. One can't help comparing them to the objects around them, like the refrigerator, the stove, and the kitchen sink. But an elephant is bigger than all of those objects, even a young elephant. And what's more, an elephant is constantly moving: flapping her ears, swinging her trunk, swishing her tail, and rocking her weight back and forth and from side to side—as if swaying to music only she can hear. Kitchens with elephants in them are overcrowded rooms.

Tua and Auntie Orchid sat down at the kitchen table—which had to be pushed up against the wall to make room for the elephant—and contemplated the problem, each in her own way. Tua cupped her chin in her hands and rested her elbows on the table, while Auntie Orchid studied the ceiling for inspiration.

"What are we going to do, Auntie?" Tua sighed.

"We?" Auntie Orchid raised her eyebrows so high on her forehead that they looked in danger of rolling over the top of her head and sliding down the back of her neck. "We?" she repeated.

"Yes, Auntie: You, me, and *chang*."

"You can stop calling her *chang* for a start," she said. "We need to give her a proper name."

"Oh, yes, please."

Naming an elephant is not as easy as it might seem. Dogs, for instance, are quite happy with just about any name you give them. And if you change a dog's name, even one he's quite fond of, he'll still come when you call. Cats, on the other hand, pay no attention whatsoever to the names we give them. They have their own names, thank you very much. That is why when you call a cat by the name you've given her, she looks at you like you'll never be capable of learning anything. "Why do I bother?" her expression seems to say.

But elephants not only expect to be named: they demand it. And they are very particular about their names. Give an elephant a name it doesn't care for, and you've got an elephant with a chip on its trunk. So you see the problem.

Growing up in the country, Auntie Orchid had known elephants that were happy with their names; and she had known elephants that were not at all happy with them. The last thing Auntie Orchid wanted was an unhappy elephant in her kitchen.

"Now before you say anything, Tua—"

"How about calling her Pohn-Pohn?" Tua suggested. "Pohn's the name of my very best friend at—"

But before Tua could finish her sentence, Auntie Orchid flipped the tablecloth over her niece's head. Flashing a grin at the elephant, she whispered, "Don't pay any attention to her. She's young, impetuous, and flighty—with an over-abundant imagination. She's only teasing, ha-ha. It's a joke. Ha-ha-ha!"

"Hey," Tua said, clawing out from under the tablecloth. "What did you do that for?"

"I think we can come up with a name that's just a *nit noi* more sophisticated than Pohn-Pohn, don't you?"

"But Pohntip's my best friend at school!" Tua explained. "And if one Pohn means happiness, then two Pohns means double happiness."

"Be that as it may . . ." trilled Auntie Orchid.

"She's happy, and I'm happy."

"Even sooo . . ."

"We're *both* happy," Tua said, looking to the elephant for confirmation.

The elephant withdrew her trunk from the cupboard and waved it over her head.

"But is Pohn-Pohn really a proper name for an elephant?" Auntie Orchid pleaded. "Look at her.

Look at those eyes. Wouldn't you just love to have eyes like that? They are positively . . . regal," she gushed. "They are a queen's eyes!"

She might have dropped to her knees and touched her forehead to the elephant's foot (which is what she imagined one did in the presence of a queen), but she restrained herself.

"She's awfully pretty," Tua agreed. "But I don't see what that's got to do with—"

"She should be named after a queen," Auntie Orchid decided. "But which one? There are so many queens to choose from. Makeda, queen of Sheba. Cleopatra, queen of the Nile. Suriyothai, queen of Ayutthaya."

Tua threw up her hands. "She's not a queen. She's like me!"

"A *pea—nut?*" Auntie Orchid gasped, before biting down on her glimmering fingernails in mock horror. (Auntie Orchid had never approved of naming Tua after a peanut, although it fit her as snug as a shell.)

"An *or—chid*?" Tua snapped back. When she saw Auntie Orchid wince beneath the cold cream and clutch her throat, she recalled her mother's words: "A sharp tongue cuts both ways."

"Orchid is a very nice name," Tua corrected herself. "We could always call her Orchid."

"Taken," Auntie Orchid cleared her throat. "Already taken, thank you very much. Two Orchids would only confuse the public, darling," she explained. "It just isn't done."

They had reached an impasse. An impasse in conversation is rather like a roadblock in traffic. It's the jam in traffic jam.

Tua hunched her shoulders, grinning impishly.

"Oh, all right. We'll call her Pohn, then," Auntie Orchid sighed.

"Pohn-Pohn!" Tua called to the elephant.

"Pohn," Auntie Orchid corrected her niece. "One Pohn is plenty Pohn enough."

CHAPTER EIGHT

A Hungry Elephant

No sooner had one problem been sorted than two more sprang to life. Pohn, or Pohn-Pohn, had opened the refrigerator door with her trunk and was searching inside for something to eat.

"What do we feed her, Auntie?" Tua asked.

Auntie Orchid turned to the elephant for inspiration and, finding none, concluded: "We're going to need some help."

In the excitement of having a hungry elephant in her kitchen, Auntie Orchid had forgotten to ask Tua what she had told her mother. "By the way, Tua, what did you tell your mother?"

"Ummm . . ." Tua shrugged.

"I'm calling her right now," said Auntie Orchid. "What should I tell her?"

"Uhhh . . ." Tua shrugged higher.

Auntie Orchid stabbed a particularly long fingernail at some numbers on her cell phone and put the instrument to her ear.

"Su-ay!" she sang out as if into a microphone. "It's Orchid here. I have Tua. We're having a girls' night. She's sleeping over with me."

Tua nodded and smiled broadly by way of encouragement. She was perfectly happy to let her auntie do this job for her.

"Here," Auntie Orchid announced, "your mother wants to speak to you."

Tua looked to Pohn-Pohn for support, but she was busy rearranging the contents of Auntie Orchid's refrigerator.

"Hello?" she managed to say into the phone.

"Hello, my cherub," replied Suay Nam. "I can't talk long. They're running me off my feet. What have you and your auntie been up to?"

Tua felt an urge to tell her mother everything, but bit her lip instead. "Nothing much."

"I've gotta go. I just got another table. Have fun. And give your auntie a kiss for me."

Tua put a kiss on the tips of her fingers and blew it across the table. Auntie Orchid snatched it out of the air and blew it back.

"Good night, my dove," Suay Nam said. "I love you the most."

"Me too. Bye, Mama." Tua closed the phone and handed it back to her auntie.

A string of sweat beaded her upper lip, and several other beads began to roll down the middle of her back. She had never kept secrets from her mother before, and didn't like the feeling.

"Never mind about your mother," said Auntie Orchid, interpreting Tua's expression. "We have an elephant to worry about."

I'll tell her everything tomorrow, Tua thought, hoping that that would ease her conscience. A conscience is like an elephant's trunk: It never rests. And a guilty conscience is particularly restless. But Tua had a hungry elephant to worry about. Her conscience would have to wait.

"Pohn-Pohn is hungry, Auntie," she said.

"Pohn is too big for my kitchen."

And so it was decided that Pohn-Pohn should be moved into the backyard, regardless of what the neighbors might say.

A temporary shelter was needed in case it should rain. And there wasn't enough food in the house to feed a hungry elephant. Someone had to go to the market before it closed at midnight.

"Sometimes the best way to stop wagging tongues is to give them a part in the play," Auntie Orchid said. "Tua, go wake the neighbors."

And go she did.

CHAPTER NINE

A Little Help from the Neighbors

"It is easier to get an elephant in a kitchen than it is to get her out again," Auntie Orchid declared to Tua when she returned from waking the neighbors.

If anything, Pohn-Pohn seemed bigger than before. How had she fit through the back door? It didn't seem possible. She couldn't turn around, in any case—there wasn't enough room. And she wouldn't back up: Pohn-Pohn was a forward-moving elephant.

The moment Tua had finished scratching her head over this pickle (for scratching the head often stimulates brain activity), a man stumbled through the back door in pajamas and slippers.

He rubbed his eyes with his fists and blinked his eyes.

"There's an elephant in your kitchen!" he declared.

"Buddha wept!" Auntie Orchid exclaimed.

"Her name's Pohn-Pohn, Uncle Yai," Tua said. "We need to move her outside."

"*Sawatdee khrap*, Pohn-Pohn," said Yai, putting his hands together and bowing a *wai*. "Better take Miss Pohn-Pohn through the house and out the front door."

Even as Auntie Orchid was throwing up her hands in protest, she realized that this was indeed the best strategy. The doors between the kitchen and the living room slid apart; and the front door, being a double door, was much wider than the back door. But she couldn't bear to watch.

"I think I'll wait outside," she said. "Tua, mind she doesn't stain the carpet."

"*Kha*, Auntie," Tua said.

An audience was gathering on Auntie Orchid's front lawn, and she stepped out on the porch and bowed.

"Where did you get the elephant?" a grinning Mr. Cham Choi asked Auntie Orchid. His wife, Mrs. Cham Choi, nodded her head vigorously to indicate that she, too, was anxious to know the answer to this question.

"A gift from the king," Auntie Orchid said, "for my community service."

"The king is truly a great and noble monarch," Mr. Cham Choi said in admiration.

"Noble and great," echoed his wife. "A most noble gift, indeed."

"Cham, darling," Auntie Orchid cooed helplessly, responding to the plan hatching in her brain, "I don't know what we're going to feed her."

"Fruit," Cham replied.

"Vegetables," his wife suggested.

"Pineapple," said Cham.

"Corn," countered his wife.

"Watermelon," said the husband between clenched teeth.

"Cucumber," said the wife out of the corner of

her mouth, as if to say: "I have more where that came from."

"Bananas."

"Lettuce."

"Sugarcane."

"Pumpkin."

"Mango."

"Tomato."

"Aha!" Master Cham exclaimed, thinking he had caught her out at last. "The tomato is a fruit."

"No it isn't," said his wife. "It's a vegetable."

Auntie Orchid had heard quite enough. "But where does one find such things?" She batted her eyes helplessly.

"The farmers' market, of course," replied Master Cham.

"Yes," agreed Mrs. Cham Choi, "the farmers' market."

"So what are you two waiting for?" Auntie Orchid wanted to know. "Hurry up," she ordered. "Pohn is a hungry elephant. Hop into your little red *songthaew* pickup and get over there before it closes. Off you go. *Reo reo,"* she clapped her hands, for the Cham Chois seemed momentarily fixed to the spot where they were standing. The claps seemed to release them from the spell they were under, and they moved as fast as they were capable of moving.

The Cham Chois' daughters, Sumalee, Kanya, and Isra, each presented Pohn-Pohn with a banana from their father's tree once she emerged triumphant through the front door. Pohn-Pohn wrapped her trunk around the bananas, one by one, and plopped them in her mouth. Then the three sisters bowed a *wai* in unison and ran back across the *soi* to fetch some more.

"What's all this?" boomed a skeptical voice. It belonged to Rungsan, the builder.

Rungsan had one good eye that worked perfectly fine and another eye that was cloudy and white. It gave him a sinister look, which was entirely undeserved. Looks can be as deceiving as a worm on a hook.

Rungsan was not a bit sinister. He was skeptical. Skepticism is a healthy muscle to exercise. A sinister nature is as unwanted as a blister. Perhaps having only one good eye with which to view the world had made Rungsan suspicious of half of everything he saw.

"This is my friend Pohn-Pohn, Uncle," Tua said, appearing out of nowhere—which is no small feat when accompanied by an elephant.

"Pohn-Pohn?" Rungsan lifted an eyebrow.

"Can you build us a shelter, Uncle?" asked Tua.

"I can build anything for anybody," said Rungsan. "But for you and your friend Pohn-Pohn, I will build a shelter fit for a queen. It will be a bamboo palace."

Tua threw her arms around Rungsan's legs, and he bowed his head and closed his skeptical eye.

When the Cham Chois returned from the market, the three sisters formed a line to hand-feed Pohn-Pohn the fruit and vegetables; Yai brought Tua a bowl of *pad Thai* noodles; Rungsan and his sons, Tam and Lin, erected a bamboo shelter with palm fronds for a roof; and Auntie Orchid, reclining in a swing chair hanging from a tree, serenaded the party with folk songs of longing, loss, and love.

Tua slept that night in a string hammock under the bamboo shelter with Pohn-Pohn watching over her.

"Sweet dreams and glad awakenings, Pohn-Pohn," she yawned, closing her eyes.

How curious people are, Pohn-Pohn must have been thinking. How creative and ingenious they are, yet capable of both kindness and cruelty. Nothing beats them for industry, that's for sure—except maybe ants, termites, and bees.

Then she reached out her trunk and drew the blanket over Tua's shoulder.

CHAPTER TEN

Beside the River Ping

The sun popped up so suddenly the next morning it left the roosters speechless. And nowhere did it burn brighter than down beside the River Ping.

Nak swept back the tent flaps and stepped outside in his bare feet. A message was waiting for him there, and he was standing in it up to his ankles.

He wriggled his toes around in the still-warm elephant dung and tried to recall what this sensation reminded him of. Still half asleep, he yawned and blinked his eyes.

It wasn't his feet that supplied the answer; it was his nose. His nose smelled elephant dung.

"What's *that* doing here?" He stared down to the ends of his legs. "Who would have . . .?"

He looked over his shoulder and glared at the tent. The tent snored back at him. He shielded his eyes and scanned the beach. . . . It was too empty. Something was missing. Hadn't he left an elephant attached to that—

"Gone!" he howled. "It's gone, Nang! Thieves! Vultures! We've been robbed!"

Nang struggled onto all fours and poked his head through the tent flaps.

"What happened? What's gone?" Then, looking down at his comrade's feet, he added: "Watch where you step, Nak. There's a big pile of dung out here."

"The elephant, you feeble-minded mud turtle!"

Nang stood up and had a look for himself.

Sure enough, the chain was empty. He was certain that that was where they had left the elephant last night.

"Maybe it's taking a bath?" he suggested.

"It's that nosy little street urchin from the square," Nak muttered. "I knew someone was following us last night. She must have made off with it while we were sleeping."

"What street urchin?" Nang asked.

"Come on," Nak ordered. "She couldn't have gotten far. I'll have my property back, or I'll have her ears."

Nang clutched the medallion he wore around his neck to ward off evil spirits. He had never liked the elephant trade, suspecting it angered the forest. Ever since Nak had won this elephant in a card game, they had been plagued by bad luck. He didn't care if he never saw it again. But Nang was a follower, and followers don't question authority. They pull up their socks and do what they're told.

He kissed the medallion and tucked it back under his shirt.

CHAPTER ELEVEN

Breakfast with Pohn-Pohn

Tua rolled over on her back in the hammock, rubbed her eyes, and stretched out her arms. When she saw Pohn-Pohn standing beside her, she squealed with delight.

"Pohn-Pohn! You're not a dream!"

Jolted awake, Pohn-Pohn reached her trunk into the hammock as if to hit the snooze alarm and catch five more minutes of sleep.

Tua gathered the trunk in both hands, hugged it to her cheek, and slid to the ground.

Pohn-Pohn blinked her eyes and flapped her ears.

"Look at you," Tua said, petting the rough and wrinkled skin on Pohn-Pohn's shoulder and ribs. "You're so beautiful."

Pohn-Pohn acknowledged the compliment with a nod.

"Oh no, Pohn-Pohn," Tua exclaimed suddenly when she saw, in the morning light, a scar worn around Pohn-Pohn's foot from the heavy chain she'd been forced to wear. Tua knelt down beside the leg and gently caressed the foot. "Does it hurt?"

It had been so long since Pohn-Pohn had been shown any tenderness that her first reaction was to recoil from the approaching hand. She had only known work, brutality, and neglect since she'd been ripped from her mother's side. But Tua's touch recalled her mother's loving caresses. She closed her eyes and allowed Tua to stroke her injured foot.

"I'll never let anyone hurt you again, Pohn-Pohn," Tua whispered. "I promise."

Pohn-Pohn opened her eyes, reached back her trunk, and gently laid it on Tua's shoulder.

"Hey." Tua's face brightened. "What do you want for breakfast? It's the most important meal of the day, although I like lunch and dinner just as much."

Pohn-Pohn might have said that mangos make an excellent breakfast, had Tua given her the chance. But it was Tua's habit to spring out of bed in the morning, race into her mother's bedroom, dive into the bed, shake her mother awake, and tell her about the dreams she'd had the night before. Mothers are more tolerant of habits like this than elephants are—especially hungry elephants. As Tua began recounting her last dream, and the one she best remembered, Pohn-Pohn turned her about with her trunk and steered her to the back of the house.

"After that," Tua continued narrating over her shoulder, "a big door opened in the floor, and you'll never guess what was down there . . ."

When Auntie Orchid entered the kitchen several minutes later, she found Tua sitting in the doorway, feeding mangos to an elephant on her back porch. She lifted the sunglasses she was wearing, squeezed her eyes together, and waited for her vision to adjust to the light.

"Good morning, Auntie," Tua said. "Pohn-Pohn really loves mangos."

At the mention of Pohn-Pohn's name, Auntie Orchid remembered how she had lobbied for a different name altogether, a queen's name, but had settled on the one Pohn (instead of two) as a generous compromise. She began to deliver an appeal to Tua to please stop employing the superfluous Pohn when using Pohn's name . . . when her memory was miraculously restored to her. Everything from the previous evening came back in an extravaganza of Olympian proportions, with herself cast in the role of the gold medal winner.

"Good morning, my darlings," she cooed, as if consoling the runners-up.

Feeding so many mangos to Pohn-Pohn had put Tua in the mood for mangos herself. But Tua didn't toss whole mangos into her mouth; chew them up, peelings and all; and spit out the seeds like Pohn-Pohn did. She preferred her mangos served with sticky rice and topped with coconut cream. Tua loved sticky rice and mango as much as she loved banana rotis with chocolate sauce and condensed milk.

When Pohn-Pohn had had her fill of mangos (which coincided with her eating the last mango in the box), Tua brought up the topic of sticky rice and mango with Auntie Orchid.

"Auntie," Tua mewed, "do you like sticky rice and mango?"

"Do I like it? I *love* it," Auntie Orchid confessed, inspecting her figure in the full-length mirror on the wall.

So it was decided that Tua should fetch two orders of sticky rice and mango from the day market at the end of the *soi*.

But that wasn't all she found at the day market.

CHAPTER TWELVE

A Narrow Escape

"We're looking for a little girl," Nak told the omelet vendor after making a quick inspection of the market. "We'll have two *pad Thai* omelets with chili sauce."

"Good morning, gentlemen," replied the vendor. "A little girl, did you say? Little girls come in many shapes, sizes, and colors. Tall, short, fat, thin; brown, pink, white, yellow, and black." He tucked the noodles into their eggy blankets, scooped them onto paper plates, sprinkled ground peanuts on top, and passed them over the cart. "That'll be thirty *baht*," he said.

Nak paid the vendor while Nang fell on his omelet like a praying mantis.

"This little girl is rather . . . short," Nak said.

"And she might be traveling in the company of a—"

"Relative," Nak finished the sentence.

"That would be our Tua. Small for a girl of ten, she is, but as smart as a watch. Stays with her auntie on *soi* four sometimes, Lady Orchid the actress. Now, I don't know if you gentlemen are patrons of the performing arts or not, but that's one show you really don't want to miss while you're in Chiang—Hey, where are you going? What about your change?"

Both mahouts had just turned away from the vendor's cart when Nang, who had been casting his eyes about for something more to eat, saw a small girl enter the market and elbowed Nak.

"Is that your street urchin?"

Nak turned in response to the elbow rather than the question (elbows speak louder than words), and was about to deal Nang a blow he wouldn't soon forget, when his gaze fell upon Tua.

Tua met his gaze and froze in midstep like a chameleon.

Nak recoiled like a cobra ready to strike, pointed a bony finger across the market, and roared:

"STOP . . . THAT . . . THIEF!"

All eyes swung from the source of the roar . . . to the pointing finger . . . to Tua . . . to the source of the roar again. But none of the pairs of eyes knew quite how to respond. They couldn't see a thief anywhere near where Tua was standing, so they froze as if waiting for someone to hit the "play" button on the remote control.

Tua took a tentative step backward . . . then another . . . and one more. The third backward step unloosed Nak like an arrow, and Tua dove into a pile of cabbages.

Vaulting over sacks of rice and stacks of plastic buckets, with Nang stumbling in his wake, Nak overturned tables and chairs, pots and pans, curry bowls and flower carts, until he reached the produce section and stood panting over the pile of cabbages. He plunged his fist into the mound, plucked out a cabbage head, tossed it over his shoulder, and began digging at the pile like a dog.

Tua was clawing her way to the back of the pile when a pythonlike grip encircled her leg. Suddenly she was dangling upside down and staring into the right-side-up face of the mahout.

"Gotcha." Nak bared his teeth and snarled.

"Put her down, you filthy brute!" cried a voice.

Nak turned to identify the speaker, a stout woman with a withering scowl and a shimmering gold tooth.

"This doesn't concern you," he snorted, shaking off the distraction. Tua wriggled in his grasp like a fish, and he had to resist an urge to smack her with a hard, blunt instrument. There were too many witnesses.

"Yes it does," said the woman. "Those are my cabbages."

"I have no interest in your cabbages. This delinquent stole my property." And he held Tua up closer to his face as if to make a positive identification.

Taking advantage of the moment, Tua reached out and gave Nak's nose a twist.

"Ai-yee!" he yelped, and released his grip.

Tua dropped onto the pile of cabbages and, rolling to the ground, squeezed through the legs of the gathering crowd and sprinted down the *soi* to Auntie Orchid's house. She had to get Pohn-Pohn out of there and be quick about it.

Just as Tua disappeared, a policeman began pushing his way through the crowd. "What's the rumpus? Can't a man eat in peace?" He pulled his cap down around his ears and plucked a napkin off his chest. "Make way," he ordered. "Step aside."

"The very man I was hoping to see," Nak smirked at the crowd. "Constable, this mob has aided and abetted a dangerous criminal. She's short, has a vicious temper, and went thataway. Approach with caution—she probably hasn't been vaccinated."

"What sort of crime?" The officer picked his teeth.

"The blackest crimes of all, sir. Theft of private property—and attempted murder!"

The crowd gasped as the officer reached for a notebook and pen. "What are the missing items?" He heaved an indifferent sigh. "Who was the alleged victim?"

"There is but one item missing. An elephant."

The crowd gasped again.

"And the victim stands before you," Nak added, pointing to his swollen nose.

"I didn't see an elephant," said the officer.

"It's probably hidden with the rest of her loot. She's a cunning little devil."

"I'll need to see your elephant's license."

"Eh? Elephant's license? Of course." Nak began to pat his pockets and look about for Nang.

Nang had melted into the crowd and was doing a less than convincing imitation of an innocent bystander.

"Nang," Nak called out. "May I have the elephant's license, please?"

"No," Nang whispered.

"Don't tell me you've left it back at the hotel?" He rolled his eyes in exasperation.

"No," Nang spoke to the ground between his feet.

"Ah," Nak said. "It must be in the hotel safe with our other documents."

He leaned closer to the policeman and murmured: "I wonder if I might have a word in private."

"Hundred *baht*," the officer replied.

"I beg your pardon?"

"Or we could go down to the station and fill out a report."

"Of course. I see. No need to bother ourselves with troublesome paperwork, eh?" Nak winked.

"What about my cabbages?" cried the woman with the gold tooth.

"And my spilled rice?" cried another.

"And my plastic buckets?"

"And my curry bowls?"

"And my flower pots?"

"One at a time," said the police officer. "One at a time."

CHAPTER THIRTEEN

On the Run

Tua tumbled through the front door, ricocheted from room to room, burst out the back, and, stopping at last with hands on knees and gasping for breath, shouted an alarm across the garden.

"They're coming! They're coming!"

Auntie Orchid was sitting in the lotus position under a bodhi tree with legs knotted beneath her on a pink and green pillow, eyes closed, and hands folded, palms up, in her lap. Pohn-Pohn, who was standing directly across from Auntie Orchid, had likewise crossed her legs and closed her eyes, and was curling her trunk in front of her face in imitation of the same pose. They each raised an eyelid and regarded the source of this interruption.

"Who's coming, darling?" Auntie Orchid exhaled. "We don't usually receive company this early in the morning."

"The mahouts," Tua shouted. "The mahouts are in the market!"

The devotees unknotted themselves and sprang into action. Auntie Orchid dashed into the house, while Pohn-Pohn trotted around the yard, looking for a place to hide.

Tua was torn down the middle. Her right foot wanted to follow Auntie Orchid into the house, and her left foot was lobbying to help Pohn-Pohn find a hiding place. Her right foot won the day. As Tua bolted for the back door, Pohn-Pohn retreated to her shelter and attempted to blend in with the scenery.

"Auntie," Tua called out as she wandered from room to room. "Where are you? What do we do? Where are we going to hide Pohn-Pohn?" Her heart was pounding like a piston inside her chest.

The door to Auntie Orchid's bedroom swung open and the actress, Lady Orchid, stepped into a shaft of sunlight shooting down from the window above the front door. She was wearing a Thai costume with bangles on her wrists and a golden crown on her head that glimmered like a temple. Batting her comely eyelashes, she turned her crimson lips up in a hint of a smile.

"*Wat*," she said.

"What?" Tua repeated.

"Not 'what,' darling," Auntie Orchid explained, '*wat.*'"

"What *wat*?" Tua asked, though she didn't think this was quite the time to be discussing temples. (She didn't think her auntie ought to be playing dress-up, either.)

"My little brother Chi Chi's *wat*, sweetie. He's being ordained as a novice monk. I've just spoken to him on the phone and he'll be expecting you."

"*Wats* have walls tall enough to hide an elephant," Tua said, warming to the plan.

"An excellent point. But you mustn't dawdle. It's a long walk to the edge of the city, with perils and traps at every turn. I'll remain behind and create a distraction while you make good your escape. It's how they do it in the movies," she explained. "What are you waiting for? Put your sneakers on. *Reo reo!*" She clapped her hands. "Hurry up, there's no time to waste. Go out the back, into the *soi*, down the street, and over the moat. It's across the bridge and just past the train station. And try not to draw attention to yourselves," she added, before blowing a kiss and sinking back into the bedroom to make up her face.

"The shortest distance between two points is a straight line," Tua reminded herself of the lesson she'd learned at school. Since point A was Auntie Orchid's back garden, and point B was Uncle Chi Chi's *wat*, a straight line between them meant crossing a very busy intersection on one of Chiang Mai's busiest streets.

She looked up one end of the *soi* and down the other.

"All clear, Pohn-Pohn," she said, trying to sound confident. But she was thinking of the "perils and traps at every turn" that Auntie Orchid had mentioned.

Pohn-Pohn reached her trunk over Tua's head and sniffed the air.

"Try not to draw attention to yourself, Pohn-Pohn," she said.

Then arm in trunk, they stepped out into the *soi*.

CHAPTER FOURTEEN

The Diversion

Nak raised his clenched fist and was about to give the door a good pounding when it fell away and Lady Orchid appeared in its place.

"Here for the show, boys?" she purred, batting her unnaturally long eyelashes.

"Oh, yes, *pleeease*," blushed Nang.

Nak bristled and shook his head like a horse. "No, we are not here for the show. We're here for our elephant. What have you done with it?" he demanded. "And where's that thieving little gutter-snipe? I'll have the law on the pair of you."

"The law? Elephants? Guttersnipes? My, but you do have a fertile imagination. You aren't by any

chance connected with the theater, are you?"

"We're street artists," Nang said, hoping to impress this dazzling creature. "Animal acts, mostly. Card tricks. I used to play the bamboo flute."

"I'll have a look for myself, if you don't mind. Outta the way," Nak said. He attempted to brush past the actress, but she blocked his way.

"I *do* mind, as it happens," Lady Orchid said, tapping his chest with a daggerlike fingernail. "Very much," she continued, walking him backward to the end of the porch. "In-*deed!*" And she flicked the end of his nose.

Teetering on the edge, he reached back his foot for a step that wasn't there . . . and toppled over like a sapling.

Lady Orchid curtsied, bowed, and blew kisses to her audience, real and imaginary.

Nang broke into applause. "What a show! What a performance! What a woman!"

"You had better see to your friend, darling," she said. "He looks a little starstruck."

"Can I come again?" pleaded Nang.

"Of course you can, you silly man. Tickets can be purchased at the box office."

Then she batted her eyes, stepped inside the house, and closed the door behind her.

"Did you see that?" asked Nang.

But Nak was lying on the ground, gasping for breath.

"Let me help you up. Are you all right? That was a nasty spill. How's your head?"

Nak pushed him away and steadied himself on wobbly legs. "She'll pay for this," he hissed.

"But I'm sure it was an accident," Nang said in her defense.

Nak's hand shot out like a cobra and bit Nang's ear.

"Ow!" Nang cried. "You're hurting me."

Nak twisted the ear another notch. "Not the woman, you mongrel half-wit! The feral brat who stole my elephant. I'll make her pay."

"You're hurting me," Nang whined. "Let go."

Nak looked down the length of his arm and drew back his hand as if from a flame.

Nang stepped away and rubbed his throbbing ear. Then, reaching for the medallion under his shirt, he mumbled an incantation.

"What's that? Speak up."

"That hurt," Nang said.

"Of course it hurt, you superstitious clod. It was supposed to hurt. How else do I maintain discipline? Now come on, if you're coming. I've got a score to settle with that brat."

Anger spread across Nak's face like a bloodstain, and Nang took two paces back.

CHAPTER FIFTEEN

The Concrete Island

After glancing over her shoulder at the empty *soi*, Tua turned back to face the bustling street ahead. Motorbikes darted past like wasps, *tuk-tuks* trolled for fares, and red *songthaew* trucks pulled up to the curbside, unloaded their passengers, and gobbled up new ones. Cars and vans bullied each other, honking insults, gunning engines, and spewing exhaust.

"We'll have to walk in the street, Pohn-Pohn," Tua said.

Pohn-Pohn raised her head and rolled back her eyes. The street roared at her like a waterfall.

"Don't worry," Tua said. "I'll walk on the outside

and protect you from the cars. Just look straight ahead and follow me."

The moment they stepped into the street, the observers became the observed. But they didn't stop traffic so much as congest it, for every car, van, motorcycle, *tuk-tuk*, and *songthaew* veered in their direction to get a better look at the unusual pair. They screeched, honked, skidded, and gawked, while Tua, walking on the outside and cradling Pohn-Pohn's trunk in her arm, stared straight ahead. As Pohn-Pohn lumbered past, every parked car cried out an alarm until the whole block was shrieking like babies in an orphanage. When they reached the intersection, Tua guided Pohn-Pohn across a lull in the traffic to a concrete island in the middle.

As Pohn-Pohn teetered on the narrow divider, spilling over into the lanes on both sides, Tua looked around her—and into the tinted windshield of a tour bus roaring down on them like a rogue wave.

A flash of sunlight reflected off the dark glass, blinding Pohn-Pohn.

"Look out, Pohn-Pohn!" Tua leapt onto Pohn-Pohn's trunk as if expecting to pull her out of the way.

Pohn-Pohn opened her eyes and, seeing Tua dangling from her trunk, tossed her head out of the lane. Her ear flapped over her eye as the bus roared past in a blur. She set Tua down on the narrow island and began inspecting her.

"I'm alright, Pohn-Pohn," Tua said, and hugged her trunk. "That was a close one." When a gap opened up in the traffic, she led Pohn-Pohn across the empty lanes and down the embankment to the riverside.

As Tua gazed across the River Ping and down to the bridge below, she wondered how she would ever get Pohn-Pohn onto a busy street again. She sat down on a hollow log to collect her thoughts and make a plan. They had to cross the river somehow, or they'd never reach the *wat*.

"We need a boat," she said. As she scanned the river for a boat or barge big enough to accommodate an elephant, Tua felt the log roll beneath her.

Pohn-Pohn's foot was on it.

"Not now, Pohn-Pohn."

Pohn-Pohn rolled the log again.

"What is it?" Tua looked Pohn-Pohn in the eye. "What's the matter?"

Then she looked over her shoulder to where Pohn-Pohn's trunk was pointing . . . and saw a sagging tent, a spent fire, and a chain attached to a stake in the ground.

The log she was sitting on was the very same log she had hidden behind the night before last.

They were back at the mahouts' camp.

Pohn-Pohn didn't wait for Tua to speak; she lifted her off the log and pulled her to the river's edge.

Tua planted her heels in the sand and pulled back on the trunk.

"We can't swim across the river," Tua said. "It's too far. It's too fast. It's too deep."

Pohn-Pohn waded into the swirling current up to her neck and, looking back over her shoulder, flapped her ears as if to say, "Come."

Tua looked up and down the river one more time, hoping for a boat to come to their rescue. There were none to be seen. So she waded into the muddy water, climbed onto Pohn-Pohn's back, clamped her arms around the elephant's thick neck, pinched her legs tight, and closed her eyes.

"Okay, Pohn-Pohn," she said. "I'm ready."

Pohn-Pohn launched herself into the swift current with her trunk rising out of the water like a snorkel.

CHAPTER SIXTEEN

In Pursuit

No sooner had Tua and Pohn-Pohn slipped over the embankment than the two mahouts came panting up to the intersection behind them. Nak stared up and down both lanes of traffic.

"Where could they be?"

"Move on, move on," said a gravelly voice. "This isn't a tourist attraction."

Nak turned around and glared down at a wrinkled old man sitting on a footstool behind a folding table. He was selling charms, medallions, amulets, and talismans. Bare-chested and wrapped in a faded sarong, he leaned over and spit betel nut juice on the ground between his feet.

Nak removed the scowl from his face. "Good day to you, grandfather," he smiled. "You didn't happen to see a little girl with an elephant go by here recently, did you?"

"Maybe I did, and maybe I didn't," said the old fossil. "What's it worth to you?"

"Worth to me?" Nak asked.

"Maybe you'd like to buy a charm, to change your luck."

"I'm not a superstitious man," Nak assured the old creature and laughed.

"Of course not. We live in the modern world. An amulet, perhaps, to ward off evil spirits?"

Nang reached under his shirt, clutched the medallion dangling from his neck, and whispered an incantation.

"What about your friend there?" The ancient nodded at Nang. "Would he like some . . . protection?"

Nang gulped.

Ignoring the questions, Nak pulled a twenty-*baht* note out of his pocket and waved it in the air.

"What will this buy me?" he asked.

"All that you desire," the old man cackled. He snatched the note out of Nak's hand, and pointed a bony finger across the street. "They went thataway."

Nak darted into the road, waving back the cars and cursing their horns, while Nang scurried after. When they reached the embankment on the other side, Nak scanned the shoreline from the bend in the river above to the bridge below.

"I don't see them anywhere," Nak frowned.

Nang saw something bobbing up and down in the middle of the river like a capsized boat. There seemed to be someone clinging to the keel. He looked back over his shoulder. The old man had folded up his table and was gone.

"What's that there?" Nak pointed to the middle of the river.

CHAPTER SEVENTEEN

Crossing the River

A wave washed over Tua and she lifted her head, gasped for breath, and opened her eyes. A swift current was plunging them downstream. Whirlpools swirled around them in fits. And they were only halfway across the river. She pinched her legs together and locked her arms tighter around Pohn-Pohn.

When they reached the deepest part of the river, Pohn-Pohn rolled over with the current, and they slowly sank below the surface.

First Tua's legs, and then her arms were torn free. She kicked and paddled through the dark, muddy water; popped to the surface and gulped

a mouthful of air; but was quickly sent spinning under the waves again. Just when she thought her lungs would burst, something grasped her ankle and pulled. She lurched through the water, leaving a trail of bubbles behind her. Tua closed her eyes—and was suddenly bathed in sunlight.

She could breathe! She was floating in air—she was flying! Then she dropped like a coconut and plopped onto Pohn-Pohn's back. Locking her legs around Pohn-Pohn's neck, Tua grabbed both of the elephant's ears. Pohn-Pohn curled her trunk back over her head and hosed Tua down.

"Cheeky *chang*," she sputtered. Then she looked back over her shoulder. With the better part of the crossing behind them, the river wasn't as scary as before—not if Pohn-Pohn was swimming with her.

Tua climbed to her feet and, standing on Pohn-Pohn's head, scanned the shoreline in search of a place to land.

"There." She pointed to an empty beach, dove into the river, and swam the rest of the way on her own.

The beach was not as empty as Tua originally thought. A committee of ducks had come down to the shore to meet them. They were lined up in a row and clapping their beaks in protest.

"*Kho thot kha,*" Tua bowed, begging their pardon. She started to offer an explanation when Pohn-Pohn emerged from the river behind her. The elephant walked through the middle of the ducks to a shallow puddle up the beach, knelt down, tipped over on her side, and began rolling in the dirt and mud. She scooped up a dripping glob in her trunk and tossed it on her shoulder.

This was more than the ducks could endure. They lifted into the air in a single body and soared out over the river like an arrow.

When Tua turned back around, she saw two men with a fishing net coming over the embankment. She waved to them, but they didn't respond. They weren't looking at her. They were looking at Pohn-Pohn.

She was thinking that she might owe them an apology as well, when they broke into a run. Before Tua lowered her arm, the men were on the beach and flinging their net over Pohn-Pohn.

"Look out for the trunk, Krit," cried the bald fisherman. "Get the net over its head."

"I'm trying, Prasong," the scrawny fisherman replied. "It's as strong as an elephant, you know."

Pohn-Pohn rocked back and forth and tried to lift her head and trunk—tried to get her legs under her body—but the net held her down in the mud. Then both men fell on top of her, and she screamed for help.

Tua set off like a rocket and, pouncing on the bald fisherman, grabbed both his ears.

"Ai-yee!" he cried, throwing his hands over his head. He scratched at Tua's arms and rolled off Pohn-Pohn's back.

Tua dropped to the ground, ran to the river, dove in, and swam away from the shore.

"Help, Prasong, quick!" called Krit. "I can't hold it by myself."

As Prasong turned to assist his friend, Tua caught the current and was swept away downstream.

Tua stayed in the current until she rounded a bend. Then she swam to shore, crept back along the embankment, and crouched down in the tall grass above Pohn-Pohn.

"What do we do now?" asked the scrawny fisherman.

"We'll sell it, of course," said Prasong. "Pound for pound, an elephant is worth more than a fish."

"But who do we sell it to?"

"To me," came an answer from atop the embankment.

Recognizing the voice, Tua flattened herself in the tall grass and caught her breath.

"Congratulations, gentlemen," said Nak. "Well done, well done. Your talents are entirely wasted on the river. You could be big game hunters."

Nak and Nang followed a narrow path down to the beach. Nang carried a heavy chain over his shoulder and an *ankus* in his hand. The sight of the *ankus*, with its pointed spike and pointed hook, made Tua shudder.

"If you just hold the beast steady while my partner attaches the chain to its foot," said Nak, "we'll gladly take it off your hands."

"Who are you?" Prasong squinted at the strangers.

"I am the owner of that elephant you're sitting on."

"What elephant? I don't see any elephant. We're fishermen. This is a fish. If you want to buy a fish, it's twenty *baht* a pound. I reckon this fish weighs, oh . . . some four hundred pounds . . . times twenty . . . that would come to . . . eight thousand *baht*," he grinned.

Krit covered his mouth with his hand and snickered.

"Come now, gentlemen," said Nak, "be reasonable. You're not exactly in the best bargaining position, are you? How did you plan on getting up? Do you have something to secure it with? Can one of you hold down an enraged 'fish' while the other goes off to fetch a chain or a rope? How long were you planning on sitting here . . . under the sun . . . with nothing to eat or drink?" He reached for a water bottle from a cloth bag slung over his shoulder, took a long pull from it, gargled, rinsed his teeth, and spat the water in the sand between his feet. "Eh?" he smiled.

The two fishermen looked at one another and shrugged.

"What about a reward, then?" Prasong wiped his bald head.

"That's more like it," said Nak. "I'm sure we can come to some arrangement."

Leaping to her feet, Tua shouted: "Nine thousand *baht*."

Pohn-Pohn cried out at the sound of Tua's voice.

The four men swung their heads to the embankment and squinted into the sun.

The elder fisherman turned to Nak and said, "That's ten thousand to you, I think."

"Don't be ridiculous," Nak snorted. "Where would a ragamuffin like that get nine thousand *baht*?"

"My auntie will give it to me," Tua said, not knowing where these ideas were coming from. "She's Lady Orchid, the actress."

"I think I've heard of her," said Krit.

"Have you got the money on you?" Prasong nodded at Nak.

"It's as close as the nearest cash machine," Nak assured him.

"The first one back with the money gets the elephant," he declared.

Tua hopped over the embankment and down the other side. She had bought herself some time. But where was she going to get nine thousand *baht*?

CHAPTER EIGHTEEN

Paying the Ransom

At the rubbish dump, Tua found everything she needed: two plastic bags—a red one and a white one—and a stack of newspapers bound with plastic twine. She sat down on a biscuit tin and began tearing off strips of newspaper, stacking them in two piles.

"What are you doing that for?" asked a voice.

Tua looked up at a sooty-faced girl who was peering at her through a gap in a chest of drawers where a drawer used to be.

"I'm making a ransom," she said.

"What's a ransom?" asked another voice. This one belonged to a small boy, also covered in soot, who was lying on a tattered mattress with his chin cupped in his hands.

"It's money you pay to get something back that's been taken away from you."

"What's it for?" asked a third voice.

Tua turned around to find another boy standing on a tire with his arms folded across his bare chest. He wore short, baggy trousers that were knotted around his waist with a tie. He was older than the other two children, and Tua hesitated before answering him.

"An elephant," she said at last. "It's a ransom for an elephant." Realizing how ridiculous this must sound, she added: "Her name's Pohn-Pohn."

"Can we help?" asked the sooty-faced girl.

And just like that, the four of them were sitting in a circle tearing newspaper into strips the size of banknotes, while Tua told them her story.

"I'm back, Pohn-Pohn," Tua called out from a distance down the beach. "And I've got the money."

Panting, the fishermen lifted their drooping heads and shaded their eyes. Prasong had wrapped his T-shirt around his head, while Krit had coated his bare neck and shoulders with mud.

"Bring it here to me," Prasong looked up and beckoned with a limp hand.

"You have to let Pohn-Pohn go first."

Tua dropped the bags in the sand, a few yards apart from one another, and stepped away from them.

"The white bag has four thousand *baht* in it," she said, "and the red bag has five. You can choose who gets the red bag."

"I do," Prasong said.

"No, me," said Krit.

After trading glances, the fishermen were on their feet and tearing across the beach after the red bag. And while they were writhing in the sand, biting, punching, and scratching each other, Tua pulled the net off Pohn-Pohn and helped push her to her feet.

"Hurry, Pohn-Pohn! Follow me."

They ran up the path, over the embankment, and down the other side. When they had reached the dry creek bed below the rubbish dump, they heard a whoop and a whistle from the top of the hill. Tua looked up and saw the three children who had helped her with the ransom waving from the roof of an abandoned car.

After waving and whooping back to them, she bowed a *wai*.

CHAPTER NINETEEN

The Other Ransom

"What a despicable child," growled Nak. He dropped a ten-*baht* coin into the cup of a limbless beggar with one hand and, just as swiftly, swiped up the cup with the other.

"She tasks me," he continued, ignoring the beggar's protests and stepping into a waiting *tuk-tuk*. Nang tumbled in after him. "To the train station. And don't spare the pistons."

After paying the driver, Nak gave Nang an extra-extra-large T-shirt to wear, carried him into the station on his back, and sat him on the floor with his arms and legs concealed under the garment. Then he stuck the cup between Nang's teeth and crept off in search of unattended luggage to rifle and pockets to pick.

Nang was content to hum his gratitude for the few coins dropped in his cup. But when a tall *farang* donated fifty *baht* to his charity, he opened his mouth to speak:

"*Khrap—*"

As the cup dropped from his mouth, Nang snapped his teeth—then his arm shot out to catch it. When it hit the floor, scattering coins and bills in every direction, he sprang into the air after them like a toad. The *farang* gaped, then frowned at this scoundrel's newly restored arms and legs.

While Nang gathered up his ill-gotten gains, all eyes—save for one pair—turned on him. Nak was lifting a wallet from the purse of a ginger-haired *farang*. He pulled out the bills and credit cards and tossed the rest in a trash can.

Two policemen appeared in the crowd as Nang beat a hasty retreat. They hadn't gotten far in their pursuit when a voice cried out in English:

"I've been robbed! Pickpocket! Somebody stole my wallet!"

A *tuk-tuk* was awaiting Nang on the road outside the train station. Nak's long arm reached out and dragged him into it.

"To the riverside," Nak ordered the driver.

Back at the beach, Nak surveyed the empty scene, then bent down and picked up a strip of newspaper the size of a banknote. The beach was littered with them.

"She's clever, I'll give her that," he hissed. "And all the worse for it. Cleverness in children is an abomination."

"It's only newspaper." Nang held up a fistful of the fake notes.

"An abomination," Nak repeated.

CHAPTER TWENTY

The *Wat*

Tua and Pohn-Pohn followed a dirt path alongside vegetable gardens, orchards, and rice paddies. Some women planting shoots in knee-deep water rose up from their work to wave straw hats over their heads.

"They're planting rice." Tua waved back. "Rice paddies are not good places for elephants to take baths in," she added, in case Pohn-Pohn might be tempted.

They met a family of water buffaloes on the path. Tua bowed to the barefoot boy following them, then asked if he knew the *wat* they were looking for.

"It's over there, *chang*," the boy said to Pohn-Pohn. He didn't seem to notice Tua at all.

"*Khawp khun kha*," Tua thanked the boy.

"*Khawp khun khrap, chang*," the boy said to Pohn-Pohn again, bowed her a *wai*, and ran off to catch up with his buffaloes.

In the distance, a glittering building loomed up from behind a whitewashed wall. A golden bell-shaped tower gleamed in the sun beside the temple.

"That's the *chedi* where the monks keep their sacred relics," Tua explained to Pohn-Pohn. "When we get inside we'll make three turns around it for luck. And to show our respect, of course," she added.

As they drew near the *wat* they could hear bells, chants, and chimes. Then a procession of saffron-robed boys with shiny shaved heads marched out of the *wat* toward them. Some were carrying workbooks and pens as if they'd just been dismissed from school.

"Look, Pohn-Pohn," Tua said. "Those boys are learning how to be good. All boys shave their heads and come to study at the temple—sometimes for

three whole months! Girls don't have to, so we must be good already."

The monks poured around them like a stream, their heads shimmering in the sun, and guided them inside the walls in a protective embrace.

Tua made three turns around the *chedi* with Pohn-Pohn following behind her. After they'd finished this ritual, a tall, slim monk in his teens approached them from across the courtyard. He was wearing sunglasses and talking into a cell phone.

"*Sawatdee khrap*, Tua," he said, bowing a *wai*. "I'm Chi Chi."

Tua bowed back a greeting.

"Your auntie's on the phone."

"*Kha*," Tua said, and put the phone to her ear. "Hello?"

"Tua, darling, is that you? Are you all right? I've been so worried. Where have you been? What adventures have you had? How's my honey, Pohn? Is she behaving herself? Isn't Chi Chi handsome? Tell me everything."

With Pohn-Pohn beside her and lending a large ear, Tua recounted their adventures after leaving her auntie's house.

"Are you hungry, Tua?" Chi Chi asked.

Tua knew that monks never eat after midday. And they never cook for themselves either. They go out early in the morning with their alms bowls and accept offerings from the people. Tua didn't know what time it was, but she knew it was well past midday.

"I'm a *little* hungry." She hunched her shoulders. It had been ages since she'd eaten. And poor Pohn-Pohn had only had a box of mangos for breakfast. "What about Pohn-Pohn?" she asked.

"We took our alms bowls to the farmers' market for Pohn-Pohn," Chi Chi said. "The people have been very generous. And we saved some of our midday meal for you. Come."

As they crossed the courtyard a temple dog awoke from her nap in the sun, stood up, barked three times at Pohn-Pohn, and fell over as if in a faint. Three more temple dogs came out of the shade to investigate, saw Pohn-Pohn, and withdrew into their crannies and nooks. Then a black and brown rooster, with a red coxcomb and coppery tail, strutted across their path as if on a dare.

Tua sat down on a mat under a shelter and was brought three covered bowls by the monks: one with soup, one with curry, and one with rice. There were piles of mangos, pineapples, watermelons, and bunches of bananas as well. Tua bowed three times to thank the people for their offerings.

"Try the curry," said a boy monk with ears like the handles on a trophy cup.

Tua filled her bowl with curry and rice, took a bite, and licked the spoon.

"*Aroy mak mak,*" Tua said. "I love it."

"My mother brings it every morning to the corner where we go for our alms. It's my favorite," the boy monk said.

"She must love you very much," Tua said.

The boy blushed with pride and wiggled his ears.

"May I feed the elephant?" he asked.

"Of course. Her name's Pohn-Pohn," Tua said. "She loves mangos the best."

Pohn-Pohn accepted a rosy-cheeked mango from the boy, tossed it in her mouth, chewed up the pulp, and spit out the seed.

As the monks stepped up one by one to feed Pohn-Pohn, Tua finished her bowl of curry and excused herself to make an offering at the temple.

Climbing the steps between the statues of two Singha lions, Tua kicked off her shoes, bowed a *wai*, and stepped over the threshold.

She walked the length of a long red carpet in the flickering candlelight, past wood carvings and shrines, until she came to a giant golden Buddha sitting on a lotus throne. His legs were folded in front of him, his right hand was draped over his right knee with his finger touching the earth, and his left hand was resting in his lap holding an alms bowl. He was surrounded by offerings of fruit, flowers, and incense. Tua knelt in front of the statue, bowed three times, chanted a prayer, and made her offering. Then she told the Buddha how thankful she was that Pohn-Pohn had come into her life. She thanked all of the people who had helped her and Pohn-Pohn come this far. She thanked the monks for taking them in and offering them refuge. "And, if it isn't asking too much," she added, "please help us find a place where Pohn-Pohn can be safe." Then she bowed three more times and withdrew from the temple.

Pohn-Pohn and the boy monks were across the courtyard and standing in front of a life-size statue of an ancient monk meditating on a platform. As Tua drew near, the statue opened its eyes and clapped its hands, sending the boys back to their chores, studies, and devotions.

Tua stopped in her tracks and bowed a *wai* to the head monk of the temple.

"Welcome," he said, after Tua had sat herself cross-legged on the ground in front of Pohn-Pohn.

"*Khawp khun kha,*" she thanked him.

"Tell me, why have you come?"

Tua began telling their story, from the moment she and Pohn-Pohn met at the fountain until they arrived outside the *wat*. Pohn-Pohn's trunk stayed draped over her shoulder the entire time.

The monk listened patiently, scarcely moving a muscle. When Tua came to the end, he blinked his eyes three times.

"What is it you wish to do?"

"Find Pohn-Pohn a home where she'll be safe."

The monk nodded. "And do you know of such a place?"

Tua thought a moment, then looked up at Pohn-Pohn for help. Pohn-Pohn flapped her ears.

"No," she said, turning back to the monk. "We don't know of a place."

The monk smiled down at this devoted pair. "There is a sanctuary in the forest not far from here," he said at last. "It is run by a woman called Mae Noi, the little mother. They have elephants there, I am told. It is a place for the sick, injured, abandoned, and abused."

Tua bolted upright. "How do we get there?"

"If it is your wish, I will arrange to have a truck take you there tomorrow morning."

Tua looked up into Pohn-Pohn's eyes and hugged her trunk.

"Yes, please," she answered for them both.

CHAPTER TWENTY-ONE

Outside the Walls

Meanwhile, a ten-wheeled truck skidded to a halt outside the *wat* walls, sputtered, shivered, and groaned. The driver cut the engine, hopped out of the cab, and waved to a waitress at the outdoor restaurant across the street.

"What's going on at the temple?" a customer asked the waitress.

"They've got an *elephant* over there," she blurted, as if revealing a secret.

"You don't say. Did you hear that, Nang? They've got an elephant at the temple."

"That's nice." Nang belched. "Can I get another beer?"

Once evening fell, two bent shapes stepped out of the shadows under the cover of night and crept along until they stood in front of the ten-wheeled truck. While one held open the hood, the other climbed on the bumper, peered inside at the engine, and began tugging at a hose.

An old dog crawled out from under the truck and sniffed at the legs on the ground.

"Go away. Shoo," Nang whispered.

The dog raised its mangy head and smiled.

Where had Nang seen that face before? As he bent over for a better look, the dog took hold of his pant leg and began to tug and pull.

"Be still, Nang." Nak pulled his head out from under the hood. "And stop that growling, or you'll wake the driver."

The old dog stopped growling on command, released the pant leg, yawned, lifted his leg, and took aim.

"Oh no," Nang said. "Don't . . ."

"Got it." Nak yanked the hose free. Then he slipped it loosely back in place and declared: "That should come off nicely."

CHAPTER TWENTY-TWO

Leaving the *Wat*

In the early morning calm, before the roosters crowed and the monks went out on their alms rounds, the ten-wheeled truck pulled into the courtyard with its headlights and taillights blazing. Tua yawned, rolled out of the hammock at Pohn-Pohn's feet, rubbed her sleepy eyes, and pulled a sarong around her shoulders against the chill.

"Look, Pohn-Pohn. That's the truck that's going to take us to the sanctuary."

Pohn-Pohn *was* looking at the truck. And she didn't like what she saw. The bed of the truck, with its wooden slats and canvas roof, reminded her of the cage she was put in when she was taken from her mother in the forest. For four days she had been imprisoned, beaten, and denied sleep, food, and water in an attempt to crush her spirit. She cried for her mother, but her mother never came.

Tua led Pohn-Pohn across the courtyard in the dark. The monks, attending to their early morning chores, moved as softly as dark shadows. When two of the monks slid a ramp out from under the truck, Pohn-Pohn stopped short and would go no farther.

"Don't be afraid, Pohn-Pohn," Tua said. "I'll be with you. Come."

But Pohn-Pohn's eyes opened wider and she flapped her ears: "No."

The driver suggested that they remove the canvas top. So four monks climbed up the slats like ants and rolled it back. But Pohn-Pohn still wouldn't budge.

Tua pleaded some more, and the monks chanted a prayer while the driver scratched his head, and looked at his watch. But Pohn-Pohn still wouldn't climb up the ramp into the back of the truck.

At last Tua gave up and sat down on the bumper. She picked up a banana that was lying on the truck bed and began peeling it. Pohn-Pohn stretched out her trunk, plucked it out of Tua's hand, popped it in her mouth, and reached for another.

"I'm sorry, Pohn-Pohn," she said. "I don't have anything else for you to eat."

Just then, the boy with the big ears appeared with a cloth bag slung over his shoulder, bulging with mangos. He stepped up on the ramp and held out a mango in his palm. Pohn-Pohn reached for the mango, tossed it in her mouth, chewed the pulp, and spit out the seed. The boy backed up the ramp and offered her another mango. She stepped up on the ramp to retrieve it. They continued that way until the bag was empty and Pohn-Pohn was standing in the back of the truck with the boy.

"You're so smart," Tua said to the boy.

"Noom," the boy answered. "My name is Noom."

Tua climbed up the ramp to join them. "You're so smart, Noom."

Noom removed a bodhi seed bracelet from his wrist and offered it to Tua. "Please accept this gift." He bowed a *wai*.

"*Khawp khun kha.*" Tua bowed back.

Noom slipped the bracelet over Tua's wrist, smiled, and wiggled his ears.

After thanking the monks, Tua waved from the back of the truck as it squeezed out of the *wat* walls and turned into the street.

The only other vehicle on the street was a motorcycle with a sidecar, and it followed the truck at a distance with the beam of its headlight.

CHAPTER TWENTY-THREE

Journey to the Mountain

As the truck rumbled beneath their feet and the wooden slats rattled around them, Pohn-Pohn wrapped her trunk around Tua's back as if holding on to a guardrail.

"Don't be afraid, Pohn-Pohn," Tua said. "We'll be there in less than an hour. It's in the forest. I've never been to the forest before. And there will be elephants there, too."

She talked and talked and talked, cradling Pohn-Pohn's trunk and looking her in the eyes, until the sun came up and they began climbing the side of the mountain.

"Look how green it is, Pohn-Pohn," Tua said, pressing her face between the slats.

The forest was mostly a dark shape, a blur, to Pohn-Pohn. But she could smell the cool mountain air above, and the warm breath of the forest beneath it.

The truck groaned up the mountainside in low gear, then raced, purring, down the other side. It climbed and fell, twisted and turned, until it came to a wide green valley surrounded by a ring of blue mountaintops. A chattering river ran through the valley, dividing it between forest and farms.

"Isn't it beautiful, Pohn-Pohn? This must be . . ." Tua started to say, when the truck began to sputter and cough. It rolled to the shoulder of the road and stopped with a gasp and a sigh.

"What happened?"

Pohn-Pohn began rocking and swaying, tossing her trunk about and flapping her ears. She looked behind her on the left, then behind her on the right.

The driver hopped out of the cab, climbed up on the bumper, opened the hood, and peered inside. Then he hopped down and came around the cab, scratching his head.

"What's the matter?" asked Tua through the slats.

"I've lost a hose."

"Oh," Tua said. "Can I help you find it?"

Just then a motorcycle with sidecar approached, slowed as if intending to offer help, then sped away and took the turnoff just ahead. The riders were wearing bright bubble helmets with black tinted visors that looked like a dragonfly's eyes.

"It must have fallen off," said the driver, turning back to Tua. "I'll have to go back to look for it. You can wait here or walk the rest of the way on foot. The sanctuary isn't much farther."

Pohn-Pohn rocked her head and tossed her trunk over her shoulder.

"We'll walk, I think, *kha*," Tua said. "Which way is it?"

"Maybe three or four miles up that river." He pointed to the valley. "The road's just there. But you might want to take the path instead, on account of the logging trucks."

"Logging trucks?" Tua curled her arm around Pohn-Pohn protectively. "I think we better take the path."

After backing out of the truck, Pohn-Pohn led Tua down the rocky embankment and onto the path below. They entered a bamboo grove and passed a riot of ferns and plants with leaves as big as an elephant's ears. A swaying coconut palm stretched so high into the blue sky it made Tua dizzy to look at it. An orchard of banana trees lined one side of the path, and papaya trees stood at ease on the other. Mangos dangled from trees like gaudy baubles. Then they stepped out into a field of corn that grew twice as high as Pohn-Pohn's back.

Pohn-Pohn reached out her trunk, plucked off an ear, and popped it in her mouth.

"Stop that, *chang*," shouted a voice.

Tua dropped the mango she was about to bite into and kicked it aside with her foot. Then she leaned over and peeked around Pohn-Pohn.

A boy with arms crossed over his naked chest and scowling like a bat was blocking the pathway. A faded sarong reached down from his waist to the tops of his two bare feet.

"*Sawatdee kha*," Tua said, stepping out from behind Pohn-Pohn and bowing a *wai*.

The boy leapt into the air like a rooster and took two steps back.

"Who are you?" he said, recovering from his surprise.

"I'm Tua. And this is Pohn-Pohn."

Pohn-Pohn ignored the introduction and reached for another ear of corn.

"Are you from the sanctuary?" the boy asked.

"No," Tua said. "But we would like to go there."

Tua was about to ask the boy for directions when she heard voices singing a chant.

"*Hoon lai ga, hoon lai ga,* where do you find a *hoon lai ga*?*"

"Quick," said the boy, "in here." He parted the cornstalks like a curtain and nodded his head inside.

"Hurry. *Reo reo.*"

Tua took Pohn-Pohn's trunk and led her inside the cornfield.

The boy straightened the stalks as best he could and covered the hole with his back.

"*Hoon lai ga, hoon lai ga,* what do you do with a *hoon lai ga*?"

Tua crept back to the path and crouched down out of sight to listen and watch.

Two children faced the boy: an older girl in a school uniform and her brother, a plump boy in a tracksuit and white sneakers. The brother kicked a dirt clod that splattered against the other boy's legs.

"What are you doing, scarecrow?" said the girl. "What do you do with a scarecrow that can't even scare crows?"

"What do you do with a scarecrow that's ascared of crows?" said her brother.

The two children laughed at the boy in the sarong.

"Afraid of crows," said the boy.

"What?" yelped the girl.

"It's 'afraid' of crows, not 'ascared' of crows," the boy in the sarong said.

"What do you know?" whined the girl. "You're only a *hoon lai ga*. Scarecrows don't go to school."

"I know what I know," said the boy.

"And that's nothing," said the girl. Then she spun around on her heels and skipped down the path singing, "*Hoon lai ga, hoon lai ga*, nobody wants a *hoon lai ga*."

"What's in there?" asked the brother, standing on tiptoes. He could see stalks swaying in the cornfield.

"A demon from the forest went in there," the boy in the sarong whispered. "With bloodshot eyes and tusks like a wild pig. Do you want to see it?"

"No!" The brother stumbled backward. Then he spit on the ground and said: "I don't believe in demons and spirits," and ran off to catch up with his sister.

"You can come out now," the boy called to Tua. "They're gone."

Tua led Pohn-Pohn back to the path, trying not to trample too many cornstalks.

"They would have told their father about the elephant," the boy said. "Farmers don't like elephants very much."

"Thank you," Tua said. "What's your name?"

"Kanchanok." He blushed and looked down at his feet.

"Why did they call you *hoon lai ga*, Kanchanok?"

"I come from a village in the hills," he said. "My father left home to look for work, and he didn't come back. Now I must work to support my brothers, sisters, mother, and grandmother. I don't have money to go to school."

"I'm sorry," Tua said.

She took off the bodhi seed bracelet and slipped it over the boy's thin wrist.

"Thank you for helping us," she said. "This was a gift from my friend Noom at the temple. My

Uncle Sip says gifts that are shared travel in a circle back to us."

Kanchanok turned the bracelet around on his wrist like a knob that opened a smile on his face.

"Would you like me to take you to the sanctuary?" he asked.

"Would you?"

"Of course," he threw out his chest. "Mae Noi is my friend. She taught me how to read and write. But we'll have to cross the river and go through the forest so no one sees us."

The motorcycle with sidecar came to a turnoff at the bottom of a hill with a sign over the road that read:

Elephant Haven

Nak stopped the motorcycle in the middle of the road and gunned the engine, attracting the attention of a gatekeeper and a chocolate-colored guard dog with a razorback.

The dog bared its teeth and growled back at the motorcycle.

"Easy, Fudge," said the gatekeeper. "Don't much like the look of them, do you?"

The motorcycle accelerated around the bend, sped up the side of another hill, and pulled over to the shoulder.

"Look there," Nak pointed his finger at the river below. "They're crossing the river with that buffalo boy and going into the forest."

"Maybe they're going to set it free in there," said Nang.

"They'll come out of the forest and cross into the sanctuary there," Nak pointed up river. "We need to get to the river and cut them off."

"How do we do that?" Nang threw up his arms. "There's a guard. And a dog."

A raft floated downriver just then with two *farangs* on board.

"By craft." He chortled, then slapped down his visor and sped off down the hill.

CHAPTER TWENTY-FOUR

Into the Forest

After luring Tua and Pohn-Pohn out of the river with sticks of raw sugarcane, Kanchanok led them into the dense forest and onto a small dirt path. The forest leaned over the path, threatening to swallow it up. A line of green tufts grew between two dusty tracks as if bursting through a seam. The tree canopy blocked out the sun, sending down long vines of grasping tentacles and shivers down Tua's spine.

When they heard voices up ahead, Kanchanok steered them off the road and into the cover of the forest.

An elephant appeared on the road, carrying a mahout behind her neck and two *farangs* in a wooden saddle on her back. The *farangs* were laughing and taking pictures of themselves. After they passed, a young elephant only a few months old came running clumsily after his mother. The mother stopped so the baby could catch up, but the mahout struck her face with a bamboo switch and ordered her to move on. She called encouragement to her calf and continued down the road with her cargo.

"Oh no, Kanchanok. We can't go there," Tua whispered.

"They're from a tourist camp upriver, not the sanctuary. Mae Noi asked them to let her take the mother and calf until he's stronger, but they said the mother must work."

Tua turned and pressed her forehead to the base of Pohn-Pohn's trunk. Pohn-Pohn blinked and hugged her back.

"Come on," said Kanchanok. "We'll be able to see the sanctuary from the ridge."

They climbed up and down the side of the mountain until they came to a clearing in the forest.

"That's it down there," said Kanchanok. "That's the sanctuary."

Tua looked down to what at first appeared to be a large farm. There were buildings and orchards, fields and gardens. But what made this farm unusual was the presence of so many elephants. There were elephants everywhere! Elephants bobbed and floated in the river. More were taking mud baths in pits on the shore. One elephant stood chest-deep in the shallows while people with buckets and brushes scrubbed it down.

"Pohn-Pohn loves playing in the mud," Tua said.

"It protects their skin from mosquito bites and sunburn," said Kanchanok.

"Oh!" Tua patted Pohn-Pohn's trunk. "Aren't you smart, Pohn-Pohn?"

"Look! That's the new baby, Mojo. He's only three months old."

A small calf with a thin tuft of black hair sprouting from the top of his head ran between the legs of his mother and auntie, his small trunk flailing in the air like a runaway hose. The skin sagged on his little body as he romped on stubby legs, flapping his ears and flicking his tail.

"He's so cute," Tua gushed.

"That's Poon under the tree," Kanchanok pointed his finger. "She stepped on a landmine in Laos and lost part of her foot. That elephant with the limp is Roy. He was hit by a truck and came here with a broken hip. And that old bull over there is Kanda," he nodded toward the river bank. "He's blind, because some men cut off his tusks with a chainsaw and it infected his eyes. Pranee and her two calves, Lucky and Mee, look after him now."

Tua swallowed a lump in her throat. "It's a hard life for an elephant, Kanchanok, isn't it?"

"Not so easy," Kanchanok shook his head.

"But they're safe now?"

"As safe as Mae Noi can make them. Come," he said, "I'll take you and Pohn-Pohn to meet her."

CHAPTER TWENTY-FIVE

A Raft on the River

The motorcycle and sidecar turned onto a dirt track and followed a crudely made sign with the words RAFTS FOR RENT painted above a crookedly drawn arrow. The track ended at a crudely made house on the bank of the river. Nak and Nang walked around to the back and lifted their visors.

There were two boys asleep in either end of a hammock as if wrapped in a cocoon. Chickens scratched at a yard strewn with bamboo poles and coconuts. A dog came out from under the porch, murmured a bark, scratched his ear, and crawled back under the house.

"*Sawatdee khrap*," Nak said to an old man in a swing chair on the porch.

The old man stared down at them, as still as a spider.

"Do you have any rafts for rent?" asked Nak. "We saw your sign on the road."

Instead of speaking, the old man tapped his cane on the floor three times.

A pig came out of the back door, followed by a man. The man yawned and blinked his eyes.

"*Khrap.*" He squinted.

"We'd like to rent a raft," said Nak.

"A raft?" He scratched his chin as if trying to recall where he'd heard that word before.

"You do rent rafts, don't you?"

"Of course. They're all out at the moment," he shrugged. "But now that I think of it, I might have one I could sell you."

"And how much would that cost me?" Nak raised an eyebrow.

"Let's see . . . I could let you have it for . . .

oh . . . say a thousand *baht*."

"A thousand *baht*?" squeaked Nak. "It's a bamboo raft, not the king's yacht."

"Handmade native crafts fetch a handsome price in the city these days," the man shrugged.

Nak pulled a note out of his pocket and waved it in the air. "Five hundred," he said. "And that's my final offer."

"One thousand," smiled the man. "And that's my final price."

Nak couldn't risk letting the elephant enter the sanctuary while he haggled over five hundred baht with this river rat. He pulled out another note and handed the money over.

"Follow me, gentlemen," said the man with a grin. "You won't regret your decision. She glides like a dream."

The old man on the porch began cackling like a mynah bird, and Nang reached for his medallion.

Standing over the raft they'd just purchased, the mahouts winced. "Does it float?" Nang asked.

"Sound as a cork," the man beamed. "Don't let appearances fool you."

"But it's a bundle of sticks." Nang nudged the raft with his foot.

"Never mind about that," Nak leapt in. "How does it work?"

"You'll need a pole to steer by. Then climb aboard, push her out to the middle of the river, and let the current do the work."

"Where's the pole?" Nak searched the ground for something to steer by.

"Did you want to buy a pole as well?" asked the man.

A cackling in the tree above sent Nang reaching for his medallion again. But it was only a pair of mynahs.

Tua, Pohn-Pohn, and Kanchanok took a narrow path along the ridge and down to a beach on the river. While Pohn-Pohn frolicked in the water, Tua sat on the bank and stared at the sanctuary on the other side.

They had made it. Pohn-Pohn's new home was just across the river—and it was beautiful over there. The elephants seemed so kind to one another. And the people seemed so kind to the elephants. Pohn-Pohn would be very happy here. She already loved the river, rolling in the current and blowing spouts with her trunk. Tua smiled. But there was a touch of sadness in her eyes.

"What is it?" Kanchanok asked, sitting down beside her. "What's wrong?"

"Nothing," she sighed. "It's just that . . . well . . . Kanchanok . . . would you look after Pohn-Pohn for me . . . when I'm gone?"

Before he could answer, they heard voices on the river and, shielding their eyes, turned to look upstream.

A raft was coming around the bend sideways. There was a man on one end stabbing the river

with a pole, and a man on the other end shouting instructions and insults. And then the raft began a slow spin, as if caught in a whirlpool.

After much paddling and stabbing with the pole, the raft corrected itself and was careening downstream nose first.

Tua sprang to her feet and shouted: "It's them, Kanchanok! It's the mahouts!"

"What mahouts?" Kanchanok asked, leaping up beside her. "Where?"

Pohn-Pohn was nowhere in sight.

Nak, who had been urging Nang to give up the pole, turned around to face downstream . . . when he saw an elephant's trunk—and then its head— rise up out of the water in front of him. It seemed to be bearing down on him like a wrecking ball.

"Turn away!" he shouted to Nang. "Turn, turn, turn!"

Nak began rocking the raft with his feet in an attempt to steer it around the elephant, but succeeded only in breaking its bonds. There were now two rafts, held together by Nak and Nang's legs. Nak leapt onto one half while Nang leapt onto the other. The two halves parted, taking separate currents around the elephant.

Pohn-Pohn whirled her trunk around her head and soaked them both as they surfed past, bouncing on the current toward the rapids below.

CHAPTER TWENTY-SIX

Mae Noi

A large floppy hat was watching from the opposite shore. The person sitting under it stood up, lifted the hat in the air, and waved it over her head.

"What have you got for me today, *hoon lai ga?*" she shouted across the river.

"That's Mae Noi," Kanchanok said to Tua. "Sometimes I bring her injured animals from the forest."

"She's so little." Tua shielded her eyes and squinted.

"She's bigger than she looks," he said. Then he shouted to the woman across the river: "What are you going to cook for me today, Little Mother?"

"Sticks and rocks and weeds, with coconut milk and red curry paste," she called back, and giggled at her own joke.

Pohn-Pohn emerged dripping from the river and approached the little woman on the shore who smelled like an elephant. Mae Noi crouched down and allowed Pohn-Pohn to inspect her with her trunk. Then she reached in her pocket and offered Pohn-Pohn a banana. Pohn-Pohn accepted the gift while Mae Noi petted and cooed over her.

Just then a sausage-shaped dog, painted brown and white like a pinto, bounded out of the tall grass and tumbled down to the shore to inspect the newcomer. She began weaving around Pohn-Pohn's legs and sniffing her feet for clues. She counted five toes on the front feet and four toes on the rear. That much was as it should be, at least.

Pohn-Pohn tossed her trunk between her front legs to say hello, but the little dog yapped at the trunk and darted out of the way. She had not finished her inspections and didn't like being interrupted. But once her job was completed, she trotted in front of Pohn-Pohn and introduced herself. Then she climbed into Mae Noi's lap and reported all that she'd learned. She did this by licking Mae Noi's face, whining, and twirling her stubby tail.

"Isn't she gorgeous, Peppy?" Mae Noi gushed.

Peppy humored Mae Noi, licking her face and whining all the more. Mae Noi had never met an elephant she didn't think was gorgeous, including cross-eyed Pinkie with the missing tail and pink ears. Mae Noi was a pushover for elephants.

Tua and Kanchanok emerged from the river and bowed a *wai*.

"This is Tua and that's Pohn-Pohn, Little Mother," Kanchanok said.

"*Sawatdee kha.*" Mae Noi bowed back. "Welcome. Are you hungry? Come," she said, taking Tua's hand, "you must tell me all about yourself and Pohn-Pohn."

The words began tumbling out of Tua's mouth as if from the pages of a book.

Pohn-Pohn fell in step behind them, followed by Kanchanok and Peppy. The little dog wound around Kanchanok's feet, jumped on his legs, and begged him to tell her all about these strangers. How had he met them? Where did they come from? Were they going to stay at the sanctuary?

Pohn-Pohn tossed her trunk up and down and from side to side. She could smell the musky scent of elephants. It was in the air and on the ground— it was all around her. She reached out and stroked Tua's back as if to say, "Can you smell that?"

Tua reached her hand behind her back and squeezed Pohn-Pohn's trunk.

They passed an old matriarch in a mud wallow with big, watery eyes. Her back was covered in a thick cake of dried mud; a wide stripe of wrinkled gray skin ran from her shoulder to her tail; then a dripping layer of bright orange mud coated her belly and legs like fresh paint. She lazily blinked her eyes at Pohn-Pohn, scooped up a trunkful of mud and grass, and tossed it on her head like a bonnet. Pohn-Pohn blinked her eyes and quickly looked away.

A young elephant with the tips of a new pair of tusks poking out of the corners of his mouth galloped past them just then, flapping his ears and flailing his trunk. Peppy yapped at the elephant for cutting them off. The elephant trumpeted a rude reply over his shoulder, ran up to the platform ahead, then looked back around at Pohn-Pohn and flapped an apology with his ears.

There were elephants coming to the platform from all directions, some with mahouts and some without. But these mahouts were different from any Pohn-Pohn had ever seen before. They walked alongside the elephants instead of driving them. None of them carried sticks, or chains, or the sharp, hooked *ankus*.

On top of the platform, people as busy as ants were sorting boxes of fruit and vegetables, hauling them to the edge, and hand-feeding the elephants pineapples, mangos, bananas, cucumbers, yams, corn, and pieces of pumpkin and watermelon as if they were pampered guests at a resort. The elephants kept coming. And so did the boxes.

Pohn-Pohn stood back, watching, listening, and smelling. It was a most unusual place.

"Who are all these people?" asked Tua, as she climbed the platform behind Mae Noi.

"They're volunteers from all over the world who have come to work for the elephants. Some are here for the day, and some stay for weeks at a time. We couldn't get along without them."

Tua had never seen *farangs* like these before. Tanned, dirty, and sweaty, they were all working— even the boys and girls!

"Volunteers come up from Chiang Mai every day in trucks and vans," Mae Noi said. "They stop at the markets along the way to collect food for the

elephants. It takes a lot of fruit and vegetables to feed this many elephants. We have our own gardens, orchards, and fields, too, so there's always plenty of work to be done. After the elephants have eaten, we take them to the river for a bath."

A pile of fur coats lifted their heads and jumped apart as they approached. Mae Noi crouched down and ruffled the heads and rubbed the bellies of four scruffy dogs.

"We're not just a sanctuary for elephants, are we, Shadow?" Mae Noi said to the shiny black dog whose ears she was scratching. "We've got dogs and cats and water buffaloes, too. All animals are welcome."

The black dog licked Mae Noi's face and yawned.

They climbed some stairs and entered an open-aired room with low tables and pillows scattered across the floor. Napping calico cats lay slung over the railings and roof beams like washing hung out to dry.

"This is where the volunteers eat," Mae Noi

said. "It's the people's feeding platform. Would you like something to eat?"

"Pohn-Pohn!" Tua exclaimed, at the same time that Pohn-Pohn called out to her. She spun around and leapt down the stairs two steps at a time.

Kanchanok crossed the platform with a branch of bananas balanced on his shoulder. "These are for Pohn-Pohn," he said.

"Thank you, Kanchanok."

Pohn-Pohn was waiting at the bottom of the steps, and Tua fell into the embrace of her outstretched trunk.

"I didn't leave you, Pohn-Pohn. I'll never leave you."

A *farang* girl and a Thai boy followed Kanchanok off the platform with a box of mangos between them. The girl had long, fine hair the color of corn silk.

"*Sawatdee kha*," she said, bowing a *wai* and handing Pohn-Pohn a mango. "What's her name?" the girl asked Tua in Thai.

"You speak Thai?" Tua couldn't believe her ears.

"So do you," laughed the girl.

"But I *am* Thai," Tua said.

"I'm Swedish," said the girl. "My name is Nikky, and that's Kit," she pointed to the boy standing behind a box of mangos with his arm draped around Kanchanok's shoulder. "He's Thai, like you."

"*Khrap*," Kit grinned.

"*Sawatdee kha.*" Tua bowed a *wai*.

"What's the elephant's name?" Nikky asked a second time. "She's so sweet."

Tua shook off her disbelief. "Pohn-Pohn. And I'm Tua."

"My mother is an elephant doctor," Nikky said, handing Pohn-Pohn another mango. "And Kit's father is a mahout."

"My mother is the best waitress in Chiang Mai," Tua said. "And my auntie is an actress."

"I'm a Thai dancer," Nikky said, and she immediately lifted her arms, curled back her fingers, tilted her head, and bent her knees.

She was so convincing that Tua could almost imagine her dressed in the costume and makeup. But before she had an opportunity to compliment Nikky, Mae Noi called down from the platform.

"Your lunch is ready in the dining area. Nikky, Kit, Kanchanok, away you go. Tua, this is for you."

"*Khawp khun kha,*" Tua bowed.

And while Mae Noi took over the job of feeding Pohn-Pohn, Tua sat down in the grass and began eating the lovely *massaman* curry.

"How is it?" Mae Noi asked.

"*Aroy mak mak,*" Tua said between spoonfuls. Then she swallowed and said, "She speaks Thai."

"Nikky, you mean?"

Tua nodded.

"She's been here a long time," Mae Noi said. "Almost four years now. She goes to the village school with Kit."

"Why doesn't Kanchanok go to the village school?"

"I'm working on that," Mae Noi said. "In the

meantime, why don't you tell me a bit more about these two mahouts."

"Will Pohn-Pohn be able to stay at the sanctuary?"

"I hope so," said Mae Noi. "But elephants are worth a great deal of money. I don't think they will give up so easily."

"But they can't take her away, can they?"

"Elephants are considered property in a court of law, Tua. If they have a legal claim on Pohn-Pohn, I'm afraid there won't be much we can do."

"Oh." Tua looked at Pohn-Pohn, and her eyes began to water. "I thought she'd be safe here."

"We'll do everything we possibly can. I promise. Now eat your curry."

As hungry as Tua felt, she found that she could not swallow another bite. It was as if a door had closed in her throat.

"Who do we have here?" called a voice from across the yard.

Tua looked up, put down her bowl, and wiped her watery eyes.

A tall, thin woman with long blond curls walked up to Pohn-Pohn and offered her a banana. After Pohn-Pohn had smelled her all over, the woman began an inspection of her own.

"This is Pohn-Pohn and Tua," Mae Noi said. "Tua, this is Margareta, Nikky's mother."

"*Sawatdee kha*, Tua," Margareta said.

"*Kha.*" Tua bowed a *wai*.

"How does she look?" asked Mae Noi.

"She's a bit underweight. I see some sores around her neck and leg, but they'll heal quickly enough. And she has scars around the insides of her ears, but they've completely healed. I don't think it damaged her hearing at all. She must have been very young when she was broken in. Those scars on her hip are newer, probably from a machete. I would say she's remarkably healthy and alert. I'll take some tests after she settles in a bit—if that's all right with you, Tua?"

"What kind of tests?"

"Blood, urine, and stool. And I'll give her a

couple of vaccinations as well. You'll let me know when you think she's ready?"

"Okay," Tua said.

"Most elephants that beg in the cities are in poor health, Tua," Mae Noi said. "It's very stressful for them. And, of course, they always run the risk of being hit by cars. They don't get any proper medical attention. We'll do as much for Pohn-Pohn as we can, in case she has to go back."

"Okay," Tua said. Then she looked at Pohn-Pohn and told her with her eyes, "I'll never let you go back."

A *farang* man ran to the edge of the platform, leaned over the railing, and called out to Mae Noi in English.

"There are two men on a motorcycle at the gate."

Mae Noi looked at Tua.

"It looks like your mahouts are here already," she said.

Tua sprang up from the ground, ran to Pohn-Pohn's side, and began scanning the grounds for a place to hide.

"They already know you're here," Mae Noi said. "There's no point in hiding."

"We'll go to the forest," Tua said.

"The safest place for Pohn-Pohn is here at the sanctuary. It could be they're only after money."

"But I don't have any money," Tua said.

"We'll see about that later," Mae Noi said. "Let's hear what they have to say."

Then she turned to the *farang* on the platform and said in English, "Tell Sekson he can let them in."

CHAPTER TWENTY-SEVEN

The Confrontation

After washing ashore downriver, the two water-logged mahouts trudged across a parched melon field and hitched a ride to their motorcycle in the back of a truck full of nervous chickens.

Nang spit a feather out of his mouth. "Can we go back to Chiang Mai now, Nak?"

Nak lifted his chin up out of his hands where he had been resting it. The clucking chickens in their cages had lured Nak into hatching a new plan. He stared across the truck bed at Nang and thought to himself, *Chickens are more helpful than he is.*

"And walk away from all that money?" he said at last. "Do you know what an elephant is worth?

No, they'll pay. They'll pay plenty." He brushed the feathers off his shoulders and chest as if preparing himself for the negotiations, then hopped out of the back as the truck came to a stop.

"What if they won't let us in?" Nang followed Nak, still worrying about the razorback dog at the entrance.

"Ha!" Nak dismissed the notion with a laugh, climbed atop the motorcycle, and motioned for Nang to get into the sidecar. "I'd like to see them try to stop me."

The motorcycle roared up one hill and down another, then crept to a stop at the entrance to the sanctuary like a cat stalking a bird.

Nak flipped up the visor on his helmet. "I'm here to collect my elephant. Open up," he ordered the gatekeeper.

Seksan the gatekeeper looked at Fudge the dog. Fudge assumed a crouch, bared his teeth, and raised the hairs on his razorback.

"Have you got an appointment?" asked Seksan.

"They'll be expecting me," Nak answered.

"Wait there." Seksan stepped inside the guard-house to make a call. A moment later he began raising the gatepost.

Nak popped the clutch and, spitting gravel, the motorcycle reared up like a stallion. Then it dropped to the ground, lurched forward, and ducked under the half-raised gatepost with Nak crouching over the handlebars. Nang was hunched in the sidecar like a toadstool. The chocolate-coated dog with the razorback fell in behind them, baying a warning to the other sanctuary dogs. Elephants began lumbering toward the main building from all directions, gathering into a single herd. A swarm of wasps shadowed the motorcycle like a dark cloud, and Nang hunched lower in his seat. Then a pair of mynahs dove across their path and Nak swerved into a ditch, came up on the other side, and nearly collided with a row of water buffaloes. He veered back down into the ditch and came up fishtailing onto the road again. After gaining control of the motorcycle, he aimed it at the building ahead and gunned the engine.

Scattering chickens and geese, they came to a skidding halt at the end of the driveway to the main building. Nak killed the motor, peeled off his helmet, and glared at the mob that stood before him. He dismounted and began walking down the length of them, inspecting all of their faces.

He stopped in front of Mae Noi.

"I've come to collect my property," he sneered. Then he leaned into Mae Noi's face and, without removing his eyes from hers, raised his arm and pointed at Pohn-Pohn.

Tua and Pohn-Pohn took two steps back as if the finger had reached across the distance and tapped them on their foreheads. Why hadn't they run when they had the chance?

"We have evidence that you've been mistreating this elephant," Mae Noi said.

"Evidence," Nak scoffed. "It's my property. I'll treat it any way I like."

"I could report you—"

"You're harboring a thief," he spat. "You're in possession of stolen property. Who are you going to report me to? The authorities? The authorities are on my side. You're the one breaking the law. If you want to keep that elephant, then you've got to pay me for it. Four hundred thousand baht."

Tua and Pohn-Pohn took two more steps back.

"I have the right to keep this elephant for as long as it takes us to conduct tests and—"

"I'm taking that elephant now, and there's nothing you can do about it. Just try and stop me." He scanned the faces looking for a challenger.

"No," Kanchanok stepped forward.

"Go back to your mud wallow, buffalo boy," Nak snarled.

Then he called over his shoulder to Nang. "Bring me the chain and *ankus*."

Nang climbed out of the sidecar, pulled off his bubble helmet, spit a feather out of his mouth, and reached behind the seat for the chain and hooked spike. As he was slinging the heavy chain over his shoulder, a ginger-haired *farang* stepped out of the crowd.

"Wait a minute," she said in English. She walked up to Nang and ran her eyes over him, as if counting his limbs. "I know you. You're that phony beggar from the train station. And you." She turned and pointed at Nak. "I remember you, too. You're the shady character who stole my wallet while he created a distraction. Somebody call the police!" she shouted.

Nak looked at Nang, who shrugged. He didn't know who this woman was or what she was talking about.

"What is this?" demanded Nak.

"This woman claims you stole her wallet at the train station in Chiang Mai yesterday," Mae Noi explained in Thai. "She's asked me to call the police.

"Margareta, would you get Chief Montri on the phone?" Turning back to Nak, she said, "I'm sure the local chief of police would like to ask you some questions. It shouldn't take long to clear this up.

A phone call to Chiang Mai to check the police report and view the videotapes, and then you can be on your way."

"You can't prove . . ."

Nak's hand rose to his breast and covered the pocket where he had slipped the *farang*'s credit cards and driver's license. He could feel them through the thin cloth, and he staggered back a couple of paces.

Several *farangs* took cell phones out of their pockets and began snapping pictures of the two mahouts.

Nak put his hands in front of his face and retreated to the motorcycle, while Nang pushed the helmet down over his head.

"You," Nak growled at Tua. "*You.*"

"I'll make sure Chief Montri gets a copy of your photographs," Mae Noi said. "And your license number."

The motorcycle roared Nak's reply, tore at the gravel beneath its tires, and hurtled screaming down the road like a whipped dog.

"Are they gone?" Tua asked.

"They're gone. And we have Shelly to thank for that."

Mae Noi turned to the ginger-haired *farang* and bowed a *wai*. "Thank you so much, Shelly. You saved the day. Tua, it looks like you and Pohn-Pohn have an American auntie."

"*Khawp khun kha*, Auntie," Tua grinned and bowed a *wai*.

Shelly bowed a *wai* back, then reached out her hand and stroked Pohn-Pohn's trunk.

Smiling, Mae Noi draped her arm around Tua's shoulder. "So, Tua," she said, "what would you like to do?"

"Do?"

"The last van of the day is leaving for Chiang Mai in half an hour. There won't be another one until tomorrow. Do you want to be on it?"

"I'd better call my mother," Tua said.

The motorcycle turned off the paved road and crawled along a dirt track to a ridge overlooking the sanctuary.

"Is that a police car down there?" Nang said. "We'll never get the elephant back now, will we?"

"An elephant isn't the only thing worth money on the black market," Nak replied.

Night at the Sanctuary

Tua hung snugly in a hammock under a shelter, while Pohn-Pohn rocked back and forth beside her as if swaying to a lullaby. Stars spattered the sky at the end of the thatched roof and then fell behind a dark silhouette of jagged mountains. An insect chorus rustled in the underbrush, and the river murmured a quiet melody.

"Mama and Auntie Orchid are coming to get me in the morning, Pohn-Pohn," Tua yawned and closed her eyes. "I don't want you to worry if I have to go back to Chiang Mai tomorrow. It'll only be for a little while. And Kanchanok will look after you while I'm gone. Mae Noi says new volunteers come to the sanctuary every day, and I can come up with them." She rolled over on her side and rested her head on her folded arm. "I love you, Pohn-Pohn. I'll never, ever"—she yawned— "leave you."

Pohn-Pohn reached out her trunk and brushed Tua's cheek. Then she rocked the hammock as if it were a cradle.

"Good night, Pohn-Pohn. Sweet dreams and glad awaken—"

Pohn-Pohn drooped her head and closed her sleepy eyes as well.

A hush fell over the fields; the river gurgled in the background; a twig snapped. A dark shadow drifted in front of the moon like a tattered cloak, blocking out the light. Nak looked over his shoulder and cocked an eyebrow. Nang opened his mouth to speak, saw Nak bare his teeth, and shrugged instead.

The two mahouts ducked behind a tool shed and listened to the silence. No footfalls, no voices, no barks. Nak looked around the corner and searched the grounds: all the buildings were as dark as cellars. His eyes stopped at the shelter across the path. He could hear the elephant and the brat breathing. Holding up two fingers to Nang, he pointed them at his eyes, and then beckoned him to follow.

With a tarp stretched between them, they swooped into the shelter like owls, tossed the tarp over Pohn-Pohn's head, looped a rope around her legs, and turned their attention to Tua.

Nang slapped tape over Tua's mouth, and Nak began spinning the hammock like a spider winding its prey in a silken shroud.

Tua's eyes opened to a blur, as if she were tumbling down a deep well. The webbing of the hammock pinched tighter and tighter, squeezing the breath out of her lungs.

"Mmmm!" she tried to scream through the tape.

Pohn-Pohn cried out, bucked, spun around, and then beat her trunk on the ground.

Abruptly, the hammock stopped, but Tua's head continued to spin. Nang began wrapping tape around Tua, binding her like a package. Nak cut the hammock down, tossed Tua over his shoulder, and ran across the field to where the motorcycle crouched hidden in the ferns.

Pohn-Pohn gripped the tarp with her trunk and tore it off her head. Then she stamped her feet until the rope loosened and fell to the ground.

Tua was gone.

All that remained was the rank smell of her kidnappers. Pohn-Pohn tossed her trunk in the air until she located where the stench was strongest and, giving one long trumpet call to let Tua know she was coming, ran into the dark after the foul odor.

Nak was handing Tua over the fence to Nang when he heard a noise coming up behind him like an ill wind. He looked over his shoulder and saw a wide swath of cornstalks toppling in the nearby field. The ground trembled beneath his feet.

"What's that?" Nang cocked an ear and squinted through the fence poles.

"It doesn't matter," Nak said, throwing his leg over the fence and dropping to the other side. "It can't save her, now. Put her in the sidecar."

Tua sucked air through her nostrils and tried to lift her head. She could see the backs of someone's legs, and the ground rushing past below her. They crossed a paved road and entered a bushy field of ferns. Then she was lifted off the shoulder and dropped into the sidecar on her back. The last thing she saw was Nak's toothy grin before a blanket was tossed over her face.

Nak raised his head in time to see the fence across the road explode into splinters. He jammed his hand in his pocket and pulled out the key, but it leapt free of his grasp and disappeared into the dense underbrush. Dropping to his knees, he began clawing at the ferns like a terrier. As Nang dashed past him, he sprang to his feet. The dark shape was bearing down fast. He turned and sprinted across the field after Nang, leaving Tua stashed in the sidecar.

A massive banyan tree sprang up out of the empty field ahead of them, its trunk flexed like a muscular forearm, its hand buried up to the wrist and gripping the ground with rooted fingers. The foliage and branches were so thick and entwined that no moonlight penetrated between them. Nak and Nang scrambled up the trunk like feral cats, climbing higher and higher into the dense, dark foliage.

Nang pulled himself onto a large bough, turned around to scan the horizon below—and came face to face with an upside-down face.

An elfish-looking man stared back at him. He had round brown eyes like polished teak, and a pointy nose and ears. He was wearing a fuzzy brown sweater and had a long black leather coat draped over his shoulders. The little man blinked his eyes, threw open his coat, dropped from the branch above, and swooped into the air on a five-foot wingspan. Then the entire banyan tree seemed to come apart as the air filled with the flapping wings and squeaking cries of a hundred flying foxes.

Shaking like a kitten, Nang crawled along on all fours, wrapped his arms and legs around the thick bough, whispered a chant, and pinched his eyes closed. Seeing the elephant quit the chase, Nak quickly climbed to the lowest-hanging branch. He was about to drop to the ground when the snapping jaws and bloodcurdling howls of the sanctuary dogs sent him scampering up the tree again.

Stuffed inside the sidecar, Tua wriggled under the blanket. "Hmm-hmm-hmm? Hmm!"

She caught her breath as a long arm reached out of the dark and drew back the cover.

"Hmmmmm!" she squirmed.

"Tua?" Kanchanok gently pulled the tape off her mouth. "What happened?"

"Kanchanok," Tua said with her first big breath. "Where's Pohn-Pohn?"

Pohn-Pohn reached over Kanchanok's shoulder, inspected Tua from the top of her head to the soles of her bare feet, slipped her trunk under her back, lifted her out of the sidecar, and sat her standing on the ground.

"Pohn-Pohn," she gasped. "I knew you would come—but the mahouts, Kanchanok! They're getting away!"

"Don't worry about them." Kanchanok began unwinding the tape from around Tua's body. "They're up a tree and won't be coming down again anytime soon if Fudge, Shadow, and Peppy have anything to say about it."

"Thank you for saving me, Pohn-Pohn." Tua stretched on tiptoes and touched her forehead to the base of Pohn-Pohn's trunk.

Nak was led away to a police car in handcuffs, but Nang, frozen with fear, couldn't be coaxed down from the tree. Two policemen climbed up and pried him loose, tied a rope around his waist, and lowered him through the branches while the volunteers and staff covered him with their flashlights.

"I'm not a kidnapper," he began confessing before his feet touched the ground. "It was him," he pointed an accusing finger at Nak. "He made me do it."

CHAPTER TWENTY-NINE

A New Beginning

The sun rose at last, chasing away the shadows, rousing the birds to song, and warming the wings of drowsy insects. Flowers lifted their faces, turned down their collars, and spread out their arms to greet the morning light.

"I'm feeling hungry, Pohn-Pohn," Tua said, responding to her rumbling stomach. She stretched and yawned. "How about you?"

Pohn-Pohn didn't need convincing. She lifted Tua to her feet and steered her toward the feeding platform. When they came upon Mae Noi sitting on a log under her floppy hat, Tua sat down beside her. She was watching an old man leaning on a stick at the edge of the pasture. He beckoned Pohn-Pohn to come to him, pawing the air with a gnarled hand.

"Who is that man?" Tua asked Mae Noi.

"That's Ek, the shaman. He lives deep in the forest and is as shy around people as a mouse deer. But because there are so few elephants living in the wild anymore, he must come to the sanctuary to talk to them."

"He talks to the elephants?" Tua gasped.

"Why does that surprise you? Don't you talk to Pohn-Pohn?"

"Yes, but . . ."

"How do you talk to her?" Mae Noi asked.

"I don't know. I just do."

"You speak to her with your heart, Tua, the same way she speaks to you. And you speak with your eyes, the tone of your voice, and the touch of your hand. The language of the heart is a tongue all of us would understand if we only took the time to learn it. And you, my little Tua, have a very big heart indeed."

"I do?"

"I've never seen one bigger."

They watched the old man talking to Pohn-Pohn and drawing his hand in the air as if illustrating a story. He cackled at the end, patted her cheek and shoulder as if dismissing a grandchild, waved his stick over his head to Mae Noi, hoisted up his sarong, and waded into the river.

"I guess I'll have to go back to Chiang Mai today," Tua said, looking down between her feet.

"Don't you want to go home?"

"I miss my mother. And I miss my auntie and all my friends."

"But you don't want to leave Pohn-Pohn, is that it?"

Tua looked up at Mae Noi and shook her head.

"I don't *ever* want to leave Pohn-Pohn."

"You may come here whenever you want," Mae Noi said. "And stay for as long as you like. We're only an hour away by car. This is your home, too, Tua."

"Thank you." Tua gave her a tight smile and looked away. She was staring vacantly across the pasture when Pohn-Pohn reached out to comfort her, and she hugged the trunk to her cheek.

"What do you want for breakfast, Pohn-Pohn?" she smiled, holding back her tears.

Pohn-Pohn nodded her head and flapped her ears, then turned Tua around on the log and gave her a nudge.

"Okay, Pohn-Pohn, I'm coming." She giggled, slid to her feet, and looked up. Her mother was standing on top of a hillock above them, looking down and smiling.

"Mama!" Tua cried, and ran into her mother's outstretched arms. Taking Suay Nam by the hand, she led her down the hillock while telling her all about the excitement of the night before.

"Pohn-Pohn saved my life, Mama," she said. "How can I ever leave her?"

"And you saved Pohn-Pohn's life, Tua," Mae Noi added, standing up from the log and bowing a *wai* to Suay Nam. "*Sawatdee kha.* Welcome. I'm Mae Noi."

Suay Nam returned the bow. "Thank you. And

thank *you*, Pohn-Pohn, for saving my Tua." She bowed again, this time to the elephant.

"This is my mother, Pohn-Pohn," Tua said.

But Pohn-Pohn already knew that by the way Suay Nam smelled, looked, and sounded. She reached out and caressed this larger version of Tua.

"Oh," Suay Nam laughed, and touched the rough skin on Pohn-Pohn's trunk.

"Can I stay with Pohn-Pohn, Mama?" Tua asked.

"But how would I ever live without you, darling?" said Suay Nam. "Who's going to find my shoes for me when they've run off and I'm late for work? Who's going to wake me in the morning and tell me about her dreams?"

"I am," Tua said. "But sometimes I'll be with Pohn-Pohn—like when I stay over at Auntie Orchid's for girls' night."

"I don't know, Tua. What does Mae Noi say? And what about school? You have to go to school."

Suay Nam pulled Tua close and hugged her, as if to keep her from slipping away.

Mae Noi spotted Kanchanok squatting in the tall grass and waved him over. He approached wearing a grin and, draping his arm over Pohn-Pohn's neck, leaned against her. She slung her trunk around his waist in a similar friendly embrace.

"This is my mother, Kanchanok," Tua said.

"*Sawatdee khrap.*" Kanchanok bowed.

"I'm glad you're here, Kanchanok," Mae Noi said. "I want you to hear this as well.

"Pohn-Pohn is going to need a mahout to look after her," she continued. "Elephants at the sanctuary choose their own mahouts, and it's pretty clear to me that Pohn-Pohn has chosen you, Tua. And since she's so fond of Kanchanok as well, I was thinking that maybe the two of you could train to be mahouts together. What do you say? Would you like the job?"

Tua swept a radiant smile over Mae Noi, Kanchanok, and Pohn-Pohn before shining it on her mother.

"Can I, Mama?"

"I don't know," said Suay Nam. "Is it really what you want to do?"

"More than anything," Tua answered.

"Mind you," Mae Noi continued, "it's a lot of hard work and responsibility. And you'll have to attend the village school and do your schoolwork as well. Come," she smiled, "let's talk about it over breakfast."

She took Suay Nam's arm and guided her toward the main building, while Tua, Pohn-Pohn, and Kanchanok fell in behind them.

"I hope you will consider the sanctuary your second home," Mae Noi said.

"Thank you. But if Tua began staying overnight at the sanctuary, I'd see even less of her than I do now. How could I bear it?" Suay Nam bit her lip.

"Tua certainly is a remarkable little girl, isn't she?" Mae Noi said. "You must be very proud."

"I love her so much," Suay Nam declared before turning her head away.

"I was wondering," Mae Noi pulled her close,

"if you would consider coming to work at the sanctuary as well?"

As they followed behind her mother and Mae Noi, Tua declared, "We made it, Pohn-Pohn! This is your home now."

Pohn-Pohn tossed her trunk about like a newborn calf. It was in the air, all over the ground, and on everything they passed: the musky scent of elephants.

"Yoo-hoo," hailed a voice from the feeding platform. "Tu-ahh, darling! Pohn, my honey! Look at the pair of you! I could eat you both up, you know I could."

Auntie Orchid descended the stairs like a monarch. The volunteers and staff followed her off the platform like flowers chasing the sun. She tiptoed across the pasture, sidestepping large piles of elephant dung, before pushing Tua's cheeks together and kissing her bulging lips. Then she hugged Pohn-Pohn's trunk and planted a pair of scarlet lips between her eyes. Tua wiped the lipstick off her mouth with the back of her hand.

Auntie Orchid then spun around to face her public, gathered niece and trunk into her arms, and struck a fetching pose.

"Don't you feel glamorous?" she crooned.

"I'm going to be a mahout, Auntie," Tua said.

Saying it out aloud seemed to make it all come true.

"That's nice, darling," said Auntie Orchid. "Every girl should have a hobby. Smile for the cameras, cherubs."

Author's Note

Toward the end of an extended trip through Oceania and Southeast Asia, my wife and I had the great fortune to walk into a restaurant, Taste from Heaven, in Chiang Mai, Thailand. The owners, Roy and Nan Fudge, passionate supporters of elephants, booked us a day trip to the Elephant Nature Park. And in less than twenty-four hours I went from being someone whose only contact with elephants had been from a distance in a zoo to someone who fed them by hand and bathed with them in a river. We met the founder of the park, Sangduen "Lek" Chailert, who explained to us the plight of the Asian elephant; her staff and volunteers; and then the elephants themselves. The next morning, back in our hotel room in Chiang Mai, I began writing the story of *Tua and the Elephant.*

It may not be possible to look an elephant in the eyes and not want to get to know her better. I hope you get the chance to try sometime.

R. P. HARRIS

DISCUSSION QUESTIONS

1. In the prologue of *Tua and the Elephant*, readers learn that due to her small size at birth, Tua is given the Thai name for peanut. In your opinion, is this a fitting name? Why or why not?

2. Describe your early observations of the relationship between Tua and her mother. Do you consider them a strong family? In what ways are they similar to or different from your own?

3. Given her mother's work schedule, Tua has a great deal of freedom to explore the night market near their home. What is it about the market that Tua finds so appealing? Do you believe it's a safe place for her? Why or why not?

4. Though the setting of *Tua and the Elephant* is the country of Thailand, there are many rituals and routines that likely feel similar to those in your own life. Considering the story, what are the elements that feel most familiar? How do these universal elements enhance the story?

5. Describe Auntie Orchid. What makes her such a dynamic character? Does she remind you of anyone you know? In what ways does her reception of Tua and Pohn-Pohn help you better understand her character?

6. Why does Tua feel so connected to Pohn-Pohn? What does her connection with this animal teach her about relationships in general? Have you ever had a close relationship with an animal or pet? What was it about that relationship that made it special?

7. Describe Nak and Nang. Though they are both guilty of mistreating Pohn-Pohn, do you find one of them to be more villainous? If so, which one and why?

8. Discuss the character traits that allow Tua to ultimately persevere. Do you share any personality traits that are similar to hers? If so, what are they?

9. Through the course of the novel and her adventures with Pohn-Pohn, Tua and her mother learn that the world as they know it will be forever changed. In what ways will it be better or worse for them? Have you had an experience that reshaped your life? In what ways have you changed due to this incident?

10. What role do the illustrations play in the story? Do you have a favorite drawing?

CLASSROOM EXTENSIONS

1. The elephant sanctuary depicted in *Tua and the Elephant* is very similar to the Elephant Nature Park located in the Chiang Mai province of Northern Thailand. Using the Internet, have students research the park to learn the following:

- *Who established the park and why was it founded?*
- *What is the park's mission?*
- *How is it supported and by whom?*
- *Besides the elephant herds, what other animals are cared for?*
- *What can individuals do to help support this facility?*

After gathering this information, have students create a visual presentation that illustrates their findings.

2. Throughout *Tua and the Elephant* important geographical locations in Thailand are referenced. Using the textual descriptions and the illustrations in the book as inspiration, place students in pairs and have them role-play as news reporters giving a report on a selected location in Thailand. To enrich the activity, record the "report" and allow students to use props and costumes for their news reports.

3. In *Tua and the Elephant*, Tua's story focuses on her connection and relationships with Pohn-Pohn and the people that matter the most to her, as well as the places she feels most connected to (the night market and later the elephant sanctuary, for example). Ask students to consider their most special relationships and their favorite places. What makes these individuals and these places so important? Have students compose a personal journal entry where they share their thoughts. Ask them to answer the following questions:

- *Who are the individuals who mean the most to you?*
- *Why are those particular relationships so special?*
- *Do you have a special place that is a sanctuary for you?*
- *What makes it so special?*
- *Do you share that place with anyone or is it something you enjoy alone?*
- *What are your favorite memories there?*

To culminate, ask for volunteers to share their writing with the class.

GLOSSARY

Ankus	A hooked stick for goading elephants
Aroy mak mak	Very delicious
Baht	Thai currency
Chang	Elephant
Chedi	Mound-like structure containing Buddhist relics
Farang	Foreigner
Hoon lai ga	Scarecrow
Khao soi	Curry noodles (Northern Thailand specialty)
Khawp khun kha	Thank you (female, sometimes shortened to kha)
Khawp khun khrap	Thank you (male, sometimes shortened to khrap)
Kho thot kha	Please excuse me
Mahout	Elephant handler
Pad Thai	Fried noodles
Pad Thai omelet	Fried noodles in omelet
Reo reo	Hurry hurry
Roti	A thin Thai pancake served with bananas, chocolate sauce, and condensed milk
Sawatdee kha	Polite greeting (female, sometimes shortened to kha)
Sawatdee khrap	Polite greeting (male, sometimes shortened to khrap)
Soi	Lane, side street
Songthaew	Covered pick-up truck with two rows of seats to carry passengers
Tua	Peanut
Tuk-Tuk	Three-wheeled motorcycle taxi
Wai	Traditional Thai greeting (slight bow, with palms pressed together)
Wat	A Buddhist temple